D1053034

HARMS' WAY

THOMAS RAYFIEL

HARMS' WAY

THE PERMANENT PRESS
Sag Harbor, NY 11963

For information, address:
  The Permanent Press
  4170 Noyac Road
  Sag Harbor, NY 11963
  www.thepermanentpress.com

Library of Congress Cataloging-in-Publication Data

  Rayfiel, Thomas, author.
    Harms' way / Thomas Rayfiel.
    Sag Harbor, NY: The Permanent Press, [2018]
    ISBN: 978-1-57962-534-4

  PS3568.A9257 T56 2018
  813'.54—dc23   2018019002

Printed in the United States of America

for Claire

1.

I am unacquainted with evil, there being no mirrors here. We shave in squares of steel mounted above the sinks. They have been kicked or punched so many times our features bear the force of the blows. It is better that way, better than seeing yourself plain. I do not want to know what I have become, if the others here are any guide.

Dinner tonight is chicken stew. Stanley, the least evolved man I have ever met, laughs directly into his plate. He giggles, taunts, drools. I will not deny I find it irritating. I have a temper. I am excitable. But I do nothing. I spoon up the slop, what was once a living creature now barely discernible from the plastic plate. (Metal has proved too dangerous, too much a temptation, to the more opportunistic among us.) Stanley's cackle rises higher and higher. The most galling part is that he does not eat. It is our one hot meal of the day. He hovers, nose almost touching the scanty portion, gleefully making a private joke *at our expense*. Or so it seems to me. But I stay calm. I perform a mental maneuver. I gnaw at Stanley's arm, his leg. My teeth delicately rip his liver. My tongue sucks the marrow from his bones. They slide lovingly from my mouth, smooth, elongated, their bumps and hollows rid of transitory flesh. His laugh is distant now, turning into the echo of a long-extinct creature. I have cured him of his disease, taken it upon myself.

And then dessert. "Pumpkin pie," a quick bread really, brown-orange squares with lots of sugar. I stuff mine into my mouth all at once, like a medication. Back in the cell, still holding it between billowed cheeks, I feel it rot the enamel off my molars. This is the closest to pure sensual pleasure obtainable here. When I swallow, the half-digested slurry bypasses my stomach and goes directly to my veins.

"Got a new friend," Cooney says.

Cooney has lost privileges. His meals, not the same as ours, are shoved through a slot in his cage. I never see what he is served. It is gone by the time I get back. He balls the cardboard box and cellophane wrap into slowly expanding spheres.

"You sure got a lot of friends."

"She's a teacher."

He shows me a picture. A homely girl, hemmed in by furniture, she holds in both hands a copy of Cooney's book, thrusting forward not the cover but the author photo on the back. His broad, good-looking Irish features laugh without a care in the world.

"Chicken," I answer, without his asking. "Chicken stew. How about you?"

I am hoping he will tell me what he eats but he never does. I am intrigued. Could it be better than what we are given? That would be unfair. He does not complain about the suspension of his privileges. If anything, being deprived seems to have made him stronger.

"From Dakota."

"North or South?"

He squints at the accompanying letter, wets his lips, and tries to decipher. The irony, or maybe you could call it flat-out disgrace, of Cooney having authored a best-selling book is that he cannot read. "But I can write," he claims, meaning talk into a tape recorder and say any fool thing he chooses, giving philosophical weight to the "spree" he went on. Despite what the critics saw as a thought-provoking existential attitude, his motives were actually quite banal. "Bitch pissed me off," he mused, lovingly turning pages when the hardback copy arrived. It was the first time he had seen the photographs, leafing through a gallery of late teens and early twenty-year-olds. "Never cared for redheads," he said about another, even though her picture was black-and-white. Then he caught me standing, peering across the corridor that divides our cells. "What are you looking at, Harms?" "You," I said. "Yeah? Well get in line," he chuckled. "They're talking about who's going to play me in the movie."

But all that notoriety does not confer upon a man the intelligence to read. I watch his mouth contort. It is the same grimace a lot of people here have, because of the antipsychotics.

"Teacher of what?"

"Huh?"

"What's she a teacher of?"

"Kids, I guess."

"Gimme that."

Reluctantly he sticks the envelope through the grate. Small objects can be passed between cells by extruding them and then blowing. It is a surprisingly efficient system. His stinky breath (Baloney sandwich? Cold pizza? Will I ever know?) gets it close enough for me to claw the paper on through.

"Don't you eat it now," he warns.

There is laughter. People are always listening. We have no privacy here. The very concept is frowned upon. Every corner, every potential shelter from prying eyes, has been exposed by surveillance cameras. The result, paradoxically, is that we are utterly alone. Everything we do or think is for show. Our true lives go on elsewhere, deep within.

I smooth the paper and make contact with . . . "Dora Moody," the signature seems to say, but is more an excuse for the pen to let loose and show what its owner truly feels. In that moment, scrawling her name, not trying to be legible, little Dora runs wild. There are squiggles, leaps. The dot of an i becomes a bird making for the horizon. My fingertips take it all in.

"She teaches kindergarten," I report. "What's a kindergarten teacher doing reading that filth you put out?"

"Maybe it makes her hot."

"She's from a small town in northern South Dakota."

"Northern South Dakota."

He makes it sound like a state of mind.

"You want me to read the whole thing?"

"No." He has lost interest. "I get the idea."

"How come they let you keep getting mail if you lost privileges?"

"That would be a denial of my constitutional rights."

I blow the letter back. She is a sad soul. Uninteresting though.

"Crow pissed himself!" someone yells.

This is followed by a bunch of ribald comments up and down the row. Stanley's baboon hoot swings through the canopy of asbestos-coated pipes and frayed electrical wires. This facility was initially described as "modern," when they still used words like that. Now it is the architectural embodiment of all our former actions. The exposed guts drip a rash-causing syrup, flake a cancerous dust. Guards are always threatening to strike because of "unsafe conditions," not the murderers, rapists, and torturers they deal with but the chemical death seeping into their lungs. Stanley's vocalizing is the background noise to this toxic jungle. The din grows louder, our cacophony responding to an unseen sunset. I search my gums for the last sweet crumbs of pumpkin pie.

Nobody talks to Crow. For the very good reason that the last person who did is no longer with us. He is of Native American origin, from the Crow tribe according to newspaper accounts, which I do not necessarily believe. I know from personal experience just how shoddy most journalistic research is. At the time of my trial I read things about me that were factually inaccurate if not wholly made up. That is one of the compensations for being locked away. We are shielded from the solar flares of lies that make everyone else's synapses go crazy. With no news, no devices, a marvelous falling-away occurs. Of course what we are left with—ourselves, our histories, the holes where our souls should be—is grim, but has a reality I almost never encountered on the outside. Indeed, the only true moments I ever spent before arriving here were in the commission of my crimes. I often wonder if they were enacted with an unconscious aim toward finding me this sanctuary from the everyday. After all, what are the alternatives? Who joins a monastery anymore?

And even if you did, if you can walk out of a place anytime what real degree of spiritual discipline are you subject to?

But Crow has gone a step further. He swore a vow of silence and then imposed it on his surroundings. You can make sport of him in his cell, as others often do. It does not seem to carry over to when we are in the yard or at meals. It is not clear how present he is. Moments do not coalesce for him. I have never seen in his eyes the light of recognition. It might be due to the pills he takes. I once saw a special doctor coming out of the dispensary when they went around with the trays. He didn't give a rat's ass about the rest of us but kept his eyes on Crow, making sure he swallowed down whatever nefarious concoction he and his pharmaceutical brethren had cooked up. So call Crow a scalp-happy bed-wetter from behind the safety of two reinforced steel walls and you are fairly safe. He will not retaliate. But do not do what Aloysius Carr did, which was to come up and whisper sweet nothings right into Crow's ear. I was not there. I was across the way. I heard it, though, and saw what everyone else saw. Odd how one simple difference, a fat, shaved, cue-ball head twisted 180 degrees, can appear so unsettling. You would think it a boon to be able to look backward, to be able to see, completely and full-on, what has taken place in your wake, but the price it exacts is your life. Everyone turned. It was the sound, not a single crack but a bunch of vertebrae, so distinct you could gauge the distance between them. Carr's arms flopped on the little patch of dirt where the blacktop runs out, trying to get themselves to face forward, to realign. It was comic. I was not the only one who laughed. But Crow, he just sat as he had before. People said they never saw him move. The authorities claimed it was a conspiracy. They could not believe that whatever happened happened too fast to see. We were in lockdown for a week.

That was how he established the silence he now takes with him everywhere. He is old, forty at least, in relation to his crimes, which took place when he was a hot-headed youth. I do not think he belongs here, or did not used to, when he first arrived. I think he was relatively normal because, of all of us, he seems the most damaged now, the least fulfilled by his journey. Others had envisioned this place, were busy creating the need for it, well in advance of the endless shackled drive and slow grinding of the outer gate, last sound you hear that does not contain the specific resonance of the interior. Crow does not "click in" the way we do. He wraps his quiet around him like an Indian blanket and sits, massive now from the antipsychotics, cross-legged, arms folded. The guards do not make their usual remarks when they pass him by. I have tried, as I said before, to find in his eyes some receptivity, but they are unresponsive to social interaction. He is stone-faced, with acne-scarred cheeks and yellow teeth. When I am in fear of losing my serenity, of falling off the spin-ning log that constitutes one's treacherous existence, I sit next to him. He smells, as everyone here does. It is the drugs. They seep through our pores. We are as hazardous as the dripping pipes, the flaking wires, the brown water. I sit next to him, almost touching shoul-ders, and feel the sheath of peace open to include me. I slip into it with a feeling of moral relief. At last a sane man, in the midst of all this dubious company. People think I am crazy to get so close. They give us a wide berth. We have not in perhaps six years (calendar units have no meaning here) exchanged a single word, but I count him a friend. And if one day he wakes from his trance and chooses to show me what takes place squarely behind my back, shows me the damage I have wrought, to the accompaniment of that ascending scale of minute bones snapping like breadsticks, well, I have seen many deaths and that would not be the worst. Not by a long way. I might even consider it, with my last thought, an act of love.

Around us, during the hour of recreation, people try shaking out the kinks their bodies have accumulated. Some walk. Others jump in place. There is no attempt at organized games, no weight-lifting or equipment of any sort. "Yard" is a misnomer, composed as it is of cracked blacktop that has been shrinking from its borders. Like a garment washed too many times it no longer covers the flesh underneath. That is what we covet, the strip of dirt between wall and asphalt, our only contact with the natural world. There are primitive benches here, a reminder of the "modern" motif that once ruled, oblong blocks of varnished wood, themselves dried and cracked and coming apart. It is another, less exalted reason I take my chances sitting next to Crow. On my own, I could not command such a prize spot. Stanley lounges on his petty throne, sitting sideways, throwing his arms and legs so he takes up an area meant for three. Outside, he is uncharacteristically somber. He looks at the sky, as we all do. We lean back, tilt our heads, open our mouths, and stare. When the occasional plane flies over, you can feel a collective sob well up in the throats of the residents.

But recreation is only an hour. With counts, proving that we are all here, at the start and finish, it ends far too quickly. Crow moves off. The cloak of silence goes with him. Temporal reality floods back. I am a bad man. It comes to me afresh in moments like this. I am flawed.

"What's she like?" Cooney asks.

"Blonde," I answer. "Dirty blonde."

"All the way?"

"All the way."

"Mind if we make it black, instead?"

"No. Why not?"

It is a game we play. It is night, but we cannot sleep. We breathe words because our cells are close enough. Talking is forbidden after lights-out. Others follow the letter if not the spirit of the rule, engaging in grotesquely frank but wordless expressions of their frustration. It is not a pretty place, a facility for offenders of our kind, after dark. With dreams that more often than not lead to screams and the occasional attempt at self-mutilation, residents try to dodge the subconscious by any means possible, crude or subtle. Cooney and I opt for the latter, collaborating on scenarios so they do not become the threadbare imaginings of one man's obsessions.

"She is up against the back seat," he contributes.

"Make?"

"Ford Bronco."

"Leather upholstery?"

"Nah."

I gather her hair in my hand, which has become immense. It holds an entire scalp's worth in one fist and exposes her face as she has never been exposed before. Eyes stretch wide, nostrils flare so they are revealed to be passageways, potential points of entry.

"Hey," he prompts.

"Rope?"

I like to throw him off the scent, not let him know what I am really feeling.

"Knife," he corrects.

"Again?"

"The butt-end. Not the blade."

"And you say, 'I can fuck you like this until you beg me to stop, and then I can *keep on* fucking you, until you beg me *not* to stop.' "

"That is poetry, Harms. Pure poetry."

I am actually rather pleased with it myself, even though it in no-wise speaks to my own condition.

Cooney whimpers a bit, but then remembers his responsibilities. He is a good player. The object of the game is to find relief at approximately the same moment.

"Now she's sticking it right in your face."

"Mmm."

"What do you do, Harms?"

I am off on my own truffle hunt, a hound, nose to the ground, tracing the root structure of an ancient oak, trained to detect that one scent where a mysterious fungus grows. Looking desperately for a way in. Panting. Paws scratching. Tail wagging.

"What do you do, Harms?"

"I assert myself."

"Damn right you do."

"I take matters into my own hands."

"Uh-huh. And here comes that train."

Male sexuality is a largely unexplored place. It is so subterranean. I tell him what I would do. Simultaneously I long to do what I cannot, what I cannot even say out loud. Indeed, I only found my true desires by performing them. Then in the act of doing, I discovered they were not my desires at all! Not in the anatomical sense. I could never purge myself of poisons. Only collect them. Prevent them from contaminating others.

He groans.

It is a soft groan, an articulate groan if such a thing is possible, in comparison to the snarls and lowings taking place all around us. I join in, chime a manufactured note in counterpoint to his own. I fake an orgasm like you read about in women's magazines. He cannot see me from where we are. I time the length of it to coincide with his. We are an old, well-adapted, married couple. There is no afterglow. No acknowledgment. It is deeply embarrassing what we do. We know it. In the undergrowth of the loud jungle night we scurry off, two insignificant mammals, taking different paths. Cooney starts to snore. I watch my hands, or stare into the absolute dark where my hands should be. My mouth is wet with a taste I cannot identify.

2.

My ministry here is under the radar. I do not want to make it public with a lot of talk. I want to take what was best from my previous world—a world in which I, admittedly, strayed from the true path—and use the skills I developed there for good. I disguise myself in the attitude of the ordinary, moving among the stunted

wounded members of my congregation, unrecognized
as their last best hope. I am learning their needs, how
to serve them, how to wash them clean. I know of no
other way to atone.

My most promising parishioner right now is Eldridge.
I chose him because he is closest to death. There is an
urgency in the need for him to acknowledge his wrong-
doings. But if I told him this out loud he would look at
me like I was crazy. He is a shifty old codger, what used
to be called a drugstore cowboy, who claims to have no
memory of his crimes. "If they say so," is the closest I
ever heard him come to admitting complicity in the trail
of mayhem he left behind. "I was out of my head."

He is only a little more in it now, his head, what
with decades spent behind various walls before being
transferred here. He is ancient enough to have been on
a genuine death row and likes to boast of having been
served two last meals.

"Really?" I ask, even though I have heard him tell it
many times before. All conversations here are repeats.
There is simply no news. "What'd you get?"

"Well, the first was a fish fry." He rubs his hands
together, remembering. "Jumbo shrimp, clams, oysters,
french fried potatoes."

I almost swoon.

"Tartar sauce?"

"What?"

"Tartar sauce? The white stuff?"

"No. Ketchup. The second meal—"

"Wait. What happened, after the first?"

"Got a stay. 11:53 P.M." He slaps his thigh, an irrel-
evant gesture. He keeps sporadic time, obeys a private
rhythm. "Second meal—"

"So you were able to eat that whole fish fry—"

"Platter. Fry platter."

"—and enjoy it? Even though you knew what was coming?"

"What the fuck," he shrugs, an enduring credo around here.

Skin has sunk into his bones. His jaw is enormous. He squints, trying to make me out through cataracts. It is hard not to mentally add a machete to his now trembling hands. It was such an exotic weapon at the time. It played an outsized role at his trial. During closing arguments, the prosecutor swung it back and forth, sending a whistling sound through the stuffy courtroom. Some contend this was prejudicial.

"Second time, I got steak but it was tough. French fries again. Creamed spinach. And hot fudge sundae for dessert. That was the best part."

"How long before you got the call, the second time?"

"Didn't get no call. Lawyer came busting in. With a piece of paper. A commutation."

His expression goes soft, reliving the moment. I cannot tell if it is gratitude at his life being spared or regret at realizing he will never have the opportunity to order a third last meal.

"They were going to let the families watch?" I ask casually.

He spits.

"You have anything prepared?"

"You mean a speech?"

We are in the yard. He is bent over, emaciated. Death has stamped its seal on him. I can feel his unease at my question.

"Maybe express remorse," I suggest. "Ask forgiveness?"

His feet perform a complicated dance step, standing still.

". . . might want to have some kind of plan in place, for when that time comes around again. It's never too late. All you have to do is—"

"I was going to shit my pants," he brightens, remembering. "That's what I was going to do. When they gave me the dose."

. . . and slaps his thigh again.

You may not call this ministering in the conventional sense, but I think I have planted a seed. You cannot be too direct here. Every word and gesture is magnified by there being so little else going on. People nurse imagined grievances, break into violence at a long-forgotten bump during the shape-up or having taken more than one's allotted forty seconds in the shower. If I can even suggest to Eldridge that he ask for mercy, just raise the possibility, maybe it will take root and blossom during those long hours spent alone in his cell.

It comes at a cost though. I walk away weak-kneed from his description of those Last Suppers. Awash in saliva, I am physically transported to the hot platter of fried food. Mentally I substitute tartar sauce for ketchup. As for the steak, my teeth ache at its toughness, but by combining each bite with a little creamed spinach and, radical as this may seem, a dollop of hot fudge, I make it more than palatable. Now they come to march me on my last walk. I do not mind. They give me the pre-drugs before the real drugs, special pills, I am told, to heighten one's mood and erase fear. Would I have anything to say? With the relatives of victims sitting beyond the plate-glass storefront window, would I have the courage to lay myself bare, truly renounce all I did, disown what made me who I am? This is the problem with being honest in one's calling. There is always an element of doubt. Or would I, like Eldridge, let my anus do the talking?

SHE IS a woman in name only. That is how she presents herself. She dresses like a man, gray pantsuit, buttoned-up white shirt, hair drawn back but not cut short. Cutting it short would be a hint of titillation. She does not understand that no matter what she wears, what attitude she assumes, the mere fact of her being here says exactly who she is. You are what you do, not whatever part you dress for. "I work with prisoners," she told us the first day, in a room lined with guards. One even had his truncheon out, patting it rhythmically. It didn't take a Freudian psychiatrist to guess what was on his mind, but she continued, oblivious, talking about data for a study, about wishing to explore our pathology and, in exchange, offering to teach us certain techniques of "mindfulness." She made it sound like quid pro quo. You tell me why you did what you did, I will teach you how to survive its aftermath, mindfully.

I do not feel bad about the abuse she was initially subjected to. That was what she wanted. I pictured her driving home, her snug little pants-suited ass rubbing against the plastic fabric of the car seat (Cooney was right, leather is too tawdry), full of all the good deeds she had done, proud of having weathered the leers and suggestive comments, of how she had held up her hand when one of the guards threatened to intervene.

"That's all right, Sergeant."

And now, on the ride home, who knows? Maybe she slips her fingers between her legs.

She did exhibit persistence. I give her credit for that. Dr. Roberta Bush, we call her, though she keeps reminding us she is not a doctor yet. We are what lies between her current status and that of a PhD. We are the data for her precious study, a last fling before she disappears into the desiccated world of academia. The world she is already dressing for.

"I've read about your case," she says.

It is our first one-on-one encounter, for which I submit to the indignity of an interrogation room, where you are turned into a piece of furniture, chained by wrists to the tabletop.

"I apologize." She sees my discomfort. "It was either this or have a third party."

She spends an inordinate amount of time going through a thick folder. If you are acquainted with my case, I feel like saying, why are you looking over it again? Especially when you have the real thing right in front of you, the genuine article. I watch her fingers turn over sheets of paper, glimpse copies of old news coverage. Her nail polish is Mango, the red-yellow blush of the fruit's skin, not its orange flesh. Fingernail polish, last bastion of sensuality, what she cannot veil in conservative clothes on her way to tease the sociopaths.

"How are they treating you?" she suddenly asks, looking up, trying to make eye contact.

"Just fine," I say to the ceiling and walls behind her.

I dislike it when people look at me. I prefer to look at them. In my world, when someone stares at you it portends no good.

"The Church of the Holy Spirit," she reads off her notes.

"What about it?"

"It's where you attended, as a boy."

"I suppose."

"You don't remember?"

"It was long ago."

"You showed a great interest then. Father Bryan, remember him? You served as an altar boy. You asked questions. Precocious questions, he said. He thought you might consider the priesthood someday."

I swerve back to her nails, trying to avoid the quicksand of her face. They are so expressive, perfectly buffed, reflecting light.

"I wonder if we could start there, at the Church of the Holy Spirit. What you remember about it. What drew you to it."

"It was just church. Where we went. I couldn't have told you the name if you'd asked. And Father Bryan, I can't believe he's still alive."

"He's only forty-five."

"Really? He seemed old to me, even back then."

"He was a young priest, starting out. And you were just a kid."

"I suppose."

"Did anything happen between you two?"

"What about mindfulness?" I ask.

She frowns. Her age is . . . what? Very difficult to say with women. They travel through time in their looks. A forty-year-old in love looks twenty. Some sour repressed teen can give a good impression of the fifty-year-old she will one day become. And there are so many gradations in between. The fact that she is not yet a doctor puts her in late twenties, I would guess. But with the flaming mango-skin color of her nails she is right back at a randy eighteen. When she starts answering my question, she could be 105.

"Mindfulness is one of the seven factors of the Buddhist Enlightenment. It's basically a way to live in the moment by detaching yourself from cravings, cravings for power, for money, for sex; even, when you reach a certain level, for happiness itself. There are a series of contemplative or, if you don't like that word, psychological exercises that you can perform, enabling you to break free of self-destructive cycles, maybe the self-destructive cycle that contributed to your being here in the first place."

"So I wouldn't be here, if I broke the cycle?"

"You would not be here in your mind," she says carefully.

It is the wrist shackles. They are cuffs looped through two reinforced holes in the table so you are almost crouched, particularly if you try using your hands to speak. The metal bites and yanks you down. It is punishment for being human.

"Would you like me to teach you one now? A mindfulness exercise?"

"I think I'd rather learn it by osmosis."

That flusters her. She goes back to the file folder, chronicle of a time I rarely revisit. I should be flattered that she made the effort, but all that wells up in me when I see those shreds of individual truths is FALSE, the word itself. Everything she has collected may be verifiable, but the picture those little bits of mosaic compose bears no relation to my memory of events. The bolted-down legs of the table give a slight squeak.

My wrists hurt. Subject control devices are cunning. They refuse to let you bleed.

"Church of the Holy Spirit," I remind her.

"Yes."

The mango blush extends to other parts of her body. I know this for a fact.

"You think Father Bryan touched me or something?"

"Did he?"

"What would it prove if he did?"

"Nothing."

"But that's what you're asking about, right from the start."

"When I spoke to him, he seemed . . . Well, he definitely remembered you."

"Of course he remembered me. I was the subject of a six-state-wide manhunt. When they caught me, they put my trial on daytime TV."

"Are you proud of that fact?"

"How can you be proud of a *fact*?"

"There is evidence of a correlation between early childhood sexual abuse and—"

"The answer to your question is no. Nothing like that ever happened."

She takes a pen out and starts writing.

"Don't you have a computer?"

"We're required to leave everything at the front office. Did you know that Father Bryan has since been accused of improper relations with several boys?"

"No." .

"He was relieved of his pastoral duties, pending an investigation."

We are staring now, despite my initial reluctance. I do not know what to think about eyes. They are neither fish nor fowl.

"How does that make you feel?" she asks. "That he may very well have been a pedophile but chose not to make his feelings known to you."

I am sweating.

"Maybe he didn't find you attractive," she offers.

They are not "windows to the soul." I have never understood why people call them that. They are alien creatures, a parasite that has grafted itself onto us, which explains their seemingly random movements, the way they dart, dilate, and contract, change color, even. What other part of our body does that? It would also explain why, when we gaze into each other's eyes, it is such a creepy feeling. Two sets of foreign-born creatures meeting in this inhospitable place, as they ride their host bodies and communicate, commiserate, in a language learned on a distant planet.

"What did Father Bryan mean when he said the questions you asked were precocious?"

"I don't know. Didn't he tell you?"

"He gave me an example. He said he once told you 'God is everywhere' and you asked if that meant when you came into a room did you squeeze a little bit of God out?"

"Not a little bit. The exact amount of God that would correspond to me. Would I displace Him?"

"See? You do remember."

"No. I'm just thinking about it now, in the present."

"But if God is everywhere, He's in you, too. So why would you squeeze a little bit of Him out?"

"He's not in me. How could God have done the things I did? I'm not God. Is He in you? Are you God?"

"I'm an agnostic."

"I thought you were a Buddhist."

"It's pretty much the same thing."

"You're not thinking clearly." I am, in spite of myself, getting excited, leaning forward, cutting off the circulation to my hands. "It's like Archimedes in his bath. If you displace a certain amount of holiness by being not-God, and if you could measure that, you would come up with a quantifiable property."

"Let's talk about your upbringing."

"No!" It amazes me how people shy away from any earnest discussion of the spiritual, much more so than they do from sex. "Don't you see what he was getting at, the ten-year-old me? Even then, I knew. God is not everywhere. He is not in us. That is why we are able to perceive Him. He is other. That is why we feel apart. It is why we have selves. Everywhere we go, we are pushing Him out, raising the level of holiness *around* us."

"What's wrong?"

I am twitching. My hand cannot go high enough to stop it, not unless I duck almost to the tabletop. Instead I try mastering the muscle that controls the whole side of my face. I know it is grotesque, the appearance I present, a parody of how a man who has committed my crimes should look, a shaking, slobbering, blinking ghoul. But I cannot help it. When I chance upon a thought that actually means something, my nervous system shifts into overdrive.

"He was timid," I say, trying to divert her attention.

"Who?"

"Father Bryan. Like maybe he knew the truth but was afraid of where that might take him."

"What truth? A truth you knew? Is that why he was nice to you?"

I laugh, or try to. It comes out as a barking gob of spit landing dead-center on her pad. She does not move, does not recoil in disgust, which impresses me. We watch the spatter-shaped drop soak into the paper.

"Tell me something more about yourself," I prompt.

She takes her pen and resumes writing.

"Where you were born, for instance."

"That wouldn't have much relevance to my study, would it?"

"Are you kidding? At least it would be a start."

"A start to what?"

"A start to explaining what you're doing here."

"I'd like to keep our exchanges professional, if you don't mind."

"It might help you understand the reason for your study's existence. And, moving backward from there, it might explain *your* existence, the path you've taken, the choices you've made."

"Do you get treatment for your seizures?"

"Spells."

"I beg your pardon?"

"They're spells, not seizures."

"What's the difference?"

The foam starts. It is more of a froth really. I try swallowing it back but that only causes it to return, with force redoubled. By now my wrists are ringed, deeply incised.

All medical care is provided within the facility. It is made clear, with no explicit announcement, that you will never leave this place except in a box. I suppose some drastic surgical procedure would be the exception. I wonder, though, at the wisdom of opening one of us up. I imagine a flock of bats flapping out, as from a guano-choked cave at dusk, nurses screaming, doctors waving scalpels, gauze-covered mouths and shower-cap-protected hair accentuating their expressions of terror. But for anything short of that we are strapped securely to gurneys in the Sick Unit.

If the main part of the facility smells, the Sick Unit's odor is even worse. It is an attempt to layer over the familiar stink—the pill-induced sweat, the excremental aroma of those who refuse to acknowledge society's basic rules—with a powerful disinfectant. I swear they must slosh that stuff on every surface, let it pool and evaporate. Breathing it makes you nauseous in a different way than the stench of the cell or yard. There lungs register an overabundance of a known atmosphere, too much of the barn. This disinfectant, ammonia mixed with gasoline, is instantly rejected by the throat as poison. But since you must, you accept it, taking in little sips of air, deeper and deeper each time until you feel unpleasantly intoxicated.

"I do not know why they continue sending you to me," Dr. Mbaéré complains. "Seizures are treatable by Dilantin, which you refuse to take."

"I hear that stuff makes your teeth hurt."

"A minor side effect."

He is giving me the most cursory of examinations. Pulse. Pupils. Heart.

"I also hear it turns you stupid."

Our contact takes place through a thin wall of latex. I like his looks: lean, with bloodshot eyes, a close yet scraggly beard. He wears a shirt and tie under a crisp white lab coat. Is he the world's worst doctor? I have often wondered. Or is this just the only job he could get, being the color of tar and having earned his degree in a country known for its atrocities?

"You may return to the general population tomorrow," he murmurs, writing on a clipboard.

"The question is, do they make me smart?"

"I am once again noting your refusal to take anti-convulsive medication."

"I mean if the drugs that stop the spells make me stupid, does that mean that the spells themselves give me some special insight?"

"I do not think, if you were so intelligent, you would find yourself here to begin with."

"You're here, aren't you?"

He pretends to see something interesting that he missed before, comes closer, and pinches a very specific area behind my knee. I scream. A knife travels in each direction, as far up as my spine, as far down as my toes.

"Sciatic nerve functioning normally," he records.

"You fucking son of a bitch."

"Are you showing aggression?"

"No."

Aggression is a code word. If you show aggression, doctors are entitled to sedate you. That stuff zonks you right out.

There are the drugs you have to take and the drugs that are optional. All of us take various mood elevators, suppressors, or antipsychotics, depending on whatever quack diagnosis we receive. Then there is a second tier, not considered essential to the maintenance of social equilibrium, which you have the right to reject. Dilantin, in my case. A third class are the "pacifiers" they pump right into your vein if you make trouble. Months can pass before your thoughts unscramble after a dose of those. Looming behind all the rest are the strange pills, the ones emissaries from drug companies deliver. They show up on our daily tray, unexpected colors, sometimes rough-hewn as if handcrafted in a mad scientist's basement. I do not know how you are chosen, which medical trial is deemed appropriate. Crow, for example. The poor bastard can't even write his own name much less report on how a regimen is working. Yet he is one of their prize guinea pigs.

Dr. Mbaéré goes about his business. From where I lie, I have an excellent view of the ceiling. The Sick Unit does not subscribe to the exposed innards aesthetic. It is more soothing and homey. People fake illnesses to get admitted here, even though they are placed in max confinement and almost die from the fumes. As a result, Mbaéré is perhaps more gruff than necessary, dealing with so much deception.

"What I'm trying to say is, I feel unusually clear-headed, once the attack is done."

His back is turned.

"Like after a tropical storm."

One of his jobs, which he must find particularly degrading, a man of his stature, a professional, is inventorying supplies. He sets down the heavy lid of a glass jar.

"Palm trees bent over," I elaborate. "Not a cloud in the sky. So all you see is blue."

"What do you know of tropical storms?"

"Nothing, I guess. Do you?"

"I know cyclones," he enunciates carefully. "Hurricanes. Typhoons."

There is a jingle of keys, then the bang of a heavy bolt being slid back. Nobody knocks in prison. The door opens. I hear a guard escorting someone in.

"Sir!" Mbaéré shouts, stiffening to an instinctive attention.

"How's our boy?" Warden asks, coming around to me.

"The patient exhibited symptoms of grand mal seizure," Mbaéré reports. "I explained to him the benefits of—"

"You gave that PhD woman the fright of her life," he smiles, looking down.

I can see two of me, staring up, twin reflections in his lenses. He is known in the corrections community as a reformer, a man genuinely concerned for the wellbeing of his inmates.

"Thank you, doctor." He cuts off the rest of Mbaéré's nervous recitation. "Why don't you go with Sergeant Lanza here and let me have a word with Harms?"

Warden has a thin, starved face. Very soulful. I always imagine him as a monk, maybe because his hair is doing that thing you see in medieval paintings, going bald on top, forming a perfect ring. He is sympathetic, to an unnatural degree, almost as if he is living our lives along with us which of course he is not. He goes home at night.

"Candidate," I manage to say.

"Who?"

"That lady. She's not a PhD yet. She's a doctoral candidate."

"Well, she was concerned. She insisted you receive medical attention. I got the sense she thought it might be her own fault, you reacting the way you did."

"I'm sorry, sir. I didn't mean to cause trouble."

"You never cause trouble, Harms." He makes it sound like a bad thing, my being so obedient, or at least cause for puzzlement. "She wanted to come back here and see how you were doing. Unfortunately that's against regulations."

"I understand."

He is young to be in his present position, in his late thirties, I would guess, not your typical product of law enforcement. Yet I heard someone say that despite his unimpressive physique he is advanced in some form of martial arts, has even competed in national tournaments. You could never tell it by looking.

"I promised I'd look in on you myself."

"Thank you, sir."

He pulls over a chair. Beyond my limited field of vision, I sense Mbaéré and the guard, Lanza, waiting on the other side of the Sick Unit. They are as far away from us as they can get.

"While I'm here, I wonder if we could have a little chat about your neighbor."

My two reflections in his glasses are subtly different. One is eager, willing to listen, while the other maintains the closed-off passive look of a lifer. I squint, wondering if it could be due to his prescription. Maybe each lens curves a different way.

"Neighbor? You mean Mrs. Mulgrew back home? She was still a nurse at the hospital when I—"

"Are you aware Raymond Cooney has filed a lawsuit against this facility? And against me personally?"

"A lawsuit? No."

He is regretful, the bearer of bad news.

"I'm surprised he didn't tell you."

"What does Raymond say you did?"

"Just about everything under the sun. Financial malfeasance. Violation of his civil rights. He'd probably accuse me of operating a whorehouse without a license if he thought he could make it stick."

"Why would he say things like that about you?"

"It's a fishing expedition. He's forcing me to produce all sorts of records and memoranda."

"What's he going to do with those?"

"Good question."

He reaches out. His hand comes to rest on my cheek. My body, despite being restrained, goes through a sensual realignment.

"You haven't done anything wrong, have you?" I ask.

"No." Again he sounds disappointed, in himself this time. "But it's costing me. I have to hire my own lawyer. You wouldn't believe what those guys charge an hour."

"Doesn't the prison—?"

"The Bureau of Prisons has its own lawyers. But the bureau's interests don't always coincide with mine. You see what I'm saying?"

I do not really. It seems none of my business. He shuffles the chair closer. His belt buckle prods my side.

"Doctor?" he calls, without looking over.

"Sir?"

Mbaéré comes hustling up.

"These seizures, when did they start? A couple of months ago? Do you have any idea what's causing them?"

Mbaéré hesitates. You can tell a lot by a man's silence. I sense, during this pause, the absolute control he must have exercised over his "patients" in whatever godless chaotic post-Colonial turd-state he hails from, as well as the similarly absolute control that was wielded over him by murderous psychotic superiors, the knife edge he walked. I suppose it makes him uniquely suited to his current position.

"Harms refuses Dilantin," he says cautiously.

"One of its side effects," I point out, "is 'mental blunting.' "

"But that kind of medication doesn't address the underlying pathology, does it?"

"No."

Warden's fingers go all diagnostic, as if they could part my flesh, expose some level beneath.

"I'm fine," I protest.

"See? There's an example. Cooney could claim in his lawsuit that I wasn't doing enough for you. That I was letting some condition progress. He could make it sound all my fault."

"That's not how it is."

"He could subpoena documents. Explore our relationship."

"What relationship?"

"You think you could run a few tests, Doctor? Rule out some of the more obvious possibilities?"

"Absolutely, sir. Possibly I would need to administer an electroencephalogram, as well as—"

"I don't want anyone poking around inside me!"

"The tests would not necessarily be intrusive."

"What I can't understand," Warden sighs, "is how Cooney could turn on us this way."

"Us?"

"The staff. The administration. We were so help-
ful, extending him all sorts of courtesies so he could
explore his creative bent. And now, when he's succeeded, succeeded far beyond anyone's wildest expectations, instead of gratitude he's gotten it into his head
to challenge us. To initiate this action."

He finally takes his hand away but continues to
stare. I try dodging his gaze. I count the black dots in
the ceiling's acoustic tile.

"National Book Award," he intones sadly.

"Only nominated."

"And now a movie."

"Just a possibility. Nothing's definite."

"Do you know that I'm scheduled to be deposed?
Under oath?"

"About what?"

"Lies. Lies people tell."

Then he shakes it off, whatever has been delaying
him. He gets up and smiles down at me from a great
height.

"I like talking to you, Ethan. It clarifies my thoughts."

"Glad to be of service, sir."

"I can count on you, then?"

"To do what?"

He gives a playful tap to the exposed hollow of my
throat.

"You have a way of encouraging people to open
up. It's a gift. Although I suppose in your previous life
it was a curse," he adds thoughtfully. "Certainly for
those you came in contact with."

"I'm not like that anymore."

"Of course you're not." He turns to Mbaéré. "Doctor,
take good care of this man."

3.

The letter has been opened, which I resent. Not
because other eyes have read what was meant for mine
alone but because the air sealed in the envelope has
dissipated. I plunge my nose to the far bottom corner
where some is more likely to have lingered and snuffle
up a bit of . . . what season is it? Fall, I imagine, from
the temperature and sky of the yard. But it is years
since I saw a tree or smelled the smoke of burning
leaves. I imagine I am inhaling a few last molecules
of virgin oxygen unsullied by the factory fumes this
place produces. I hold them deep in my lungs as if they
could undo a billion breaths' worth of damage.

It is from Mother. She is my only correspondent.
We both act as if I have done nothing wrong, merely
gone away for a time, during which she is duty bound
to keep me informed.

*The temperature today is 72 degrees. I had a half gallon
of Ruby Red Port on the high shelf behind the cleaning supplies but when I stood on a chair to reach it there must have
been a hole because half the bottle was missing.*

Half the bottle. I see it sliced down the middle, one
whole side of glass gone, yet the contents miraculously
intact, a ruby red wall shimmering in space. That is
how removed the simplest descriptions of domestic life
have become for me.

The rest of the letter is full of similar observa-
tions. I hold it close to my eyes, trying to nestle in the
path of her ballpoint pen. That hole in the bottle is, of
course, her throat. She hides wine behind the cleaning

supplies in a cunning attempt to outwit herself. Once, already in a stupor from what some afternoon caller had brought, she took a healthy swig of liquid bleach and spent three days in the hospital. The worst part, she claimed, was how they assumed it had been an act of self-destruction.

"Why would I do a thing like that?" she appealed.

But now she has mellowed. She is older and has simplified her needs. Perhaps it also has to do with the knowledge that I am no longer there to find her on the floor, call the operator, and read off the bottle "Mr. Clean," confusing that housewife's fantasy of a gypsy lover with the fat businessman who had recently hitched his belt and left, taking his Southern Comfort with him.

The checkout girl at Star Market was not dressed properly. When I asked why she was not wearing a bra the little bitch had the nerve to tell me the material of her shirt was 'stretchy.' I told her by the time she was 30 her breasts would look like a pair of milk bottles.

Star Market, where I once ran through the swinging doors at the back of the meat section. A man was standing over a massive butcher's block carving up a lamb. The shape was still visible, headless and skinned, blue and glistening. His knife did not so much cut as seek out weakness. The carcass fell magically apart, or so I fantasized in the minute before I was spotted and roughly escorted back to the brightly lit, jingle-thick falsity of the retail area. But for a moment I had glimpsed and been irrevocably changed by a vision of the ritual slaughter that underlies the mundane acts of our waking lives, the Black Mass that gives them meaning.

Star Market. Odd she brings it up. I toy with the idea we connect on some level, that she remembers an incident so crucial to me, but in the end reject the notion. Her intentions lie elsewhere. She is castigating her former self, the checkout girl. She is the slut-turned-lush-turned-censorious-matron, as inevitable a progression as my own.

I read the rest of the letter, bringing it closer and closer to my face. By the end I am not so much deciphering the banal words as riding the loops of her handwriting, the ups-and-downs of our life together. Then I am swallowing it, the stiff notepaper she buys, a genteel protest against her life of squalor. I chew, grind the wood pulp between my molars, feel it shudder down my esophagus. The acid of my stomach squirts. I cheer as lingering dust mites and other organisms are incinerated back to their constituent atoms.

Yet there is something peculiar about the taste of her penmanship. It does not provide the usual comfort.

"You up for this?" Cooney asks.

"—much as I'll ever be."

He blows over several sheets, heavily redacted by the authorities. His most precious possession, an ancient cassette tape recorder, is at the ready.

I look at the questions. They are being posed by a national magazine. The reporter was denied access "due to the prisoner's continual flouting of regulations," an unnamed official is quoted in the run-up to the Q&A.

"How has the reception of *Rocky Mountain Fever* changed your life?" I read.

"It hasn't," he promptly answers. His egotism is so vast he does not bother to pitch his voice across

the space. Rather, he croons into the handheld microphone. "It only confirmed what I already knew to be
true. When I won that prize, it was like—"

"You didn't win," I interrupt. "You were nominated."

"—the world made sense, finally. It had caught up
with me. With my way of looking at things."

The next question is crossed out. Where do they
get such a wide-tipped marker? I wonder, trying to see
past the black swathe.

"Yo!" he yells, recalling me to the present.

"Several victims organizations have demanded a
boycott of your publishing house. Do you understand
their concerns?"

"I don't know why they form these groups," he
sighs. Everything takes on the tone of a sleazy pick-
up scene with him. "If they have an issue, they should
take it up with me directly. I answer every piece of
mail I get."

I snort. That is patently untrue.

"But when people get together in a big group, and
let that group speak for them, they lose their manatee."

"Their what?"

"Their manatee."

"Their *hu*manity."

"No. Humanity is humanity in general. But if it's
mine alone, it's just that. My manatee."

"Suit yourself."

He carefully goes back to record over our unscripted
exchange. In his own way he is quite professional. He
clears his throat, signaling for me to continue.

"Why were all your victims white?"

"Well"—he seems slightly offended—"I don't think
of people in terms of their color. I think race hatred is a

great source of misery in this country. It's like that man said, 'Why can't we all just get along?' He was black, wasn't he?"

. . . you want to come on back to my place? I can almost hear him adding, had this been ten years ago, at a biker bar or the beer tent of a fairground. Those would be the last words some poor misguided runaway would ever hear.

"What is life like in prison? What is your daily routine?"

"Exercise and contemplation."

"Exercise? They don't even let you in the yard."

"I find thinking a physical act," he explains into the tape recorder. "Always have. So even though they have caged my body I stay fit by a series of mental calisthenics, performed within the limitless freedom of my mind."

"What are you served for dinner each night?"

"I am given—" He frowns and looks over. "That's not on the list. You made that one up."

"Might be interesting. Readers like to know stuff like that."

"You'd make a piss-poor reporter, Harms. Is that all there is?"

"The rest are crossed out."

"Bastards."

He goes about composing an indignant cover letter to the cassette he will now send off. It is a sight to behold, Cooney writing, but he will not let anyone else do it. He is paranoid about false statements being made in his name. He licks the end of a stubby pencil (pens are not permitted, they too bear the stigma of being potential weapons) and prints in block letters a few simple misspelled words, one feeble scratch at a time, pausing and holding the page away from himself as if he were Michelangelo admiring a masterpiece in progress.

"Got a letter from Tucson," he says, feeling my stare. "Barmaid. It came with a nightie."

"What's this lawsuit I hear you filed?"

"Said she slept in it for a week first. To break it in. Very considerate."

I squint around his cell.

"I don't see no nightie."

"You're looking at it."

He wriggles a bit, to demonstrate.

"You trying to get them to reopen your case?"

"Little tight around the tits."

"Or is it about them taking away your privileges?"

He frowns and looks up, seeming to notice me for the first time.

"What's it to you?"

"Nothing." I brood over the contents of my own communication. "Mother sounds a little confused."

"Your mother," he manages to write and answer at the same time, "can take care of herself."

"Not really. I was always the responsible one."

"Exactly. 'Responsible.' And look where it landed you. While she's still living on Easy Street."

"Bangetter Road," I correct, though I know what he means.

"Anything she gets, she got coming."

"You don't even know her."

"Oh, I know your mother." He finishes his pathetic excuse for a letter and reaches for the padded envelope. "I known your mother all my life."

He is jealous, never having had the advantages of maternal affection. He spent his entire childhood in a Home For Wayward Boys. It wasn't called that anymore, of course, but the words themselves were still chiseled over the entrance to the main building. They endure, are permanently carved into his forehead, I imagine.

"They're never going to let you out, you know. No matter how many lawyers you hire."

"I'm not looking to get out."

"Then what's the point?"

He ignores the question.

"She's easily taken advantage of," I sigh.

". . . stop worrying about your mama."

Later, some time in the early hours, I become aware that Cooney is having a nightmare. He yelps, sobs, tries to tear himself free, perhaps of the constricting nightie his smitten reader has sent. I hear him beg and plead. He cowers as if pursued by wolves, then begins to gag. I watch with detached interest. It never occurs to me to call over and try rescuing him. It is not from lack of caring. On the contrary, if there is anyone I do care about in this dump it is Raymond Cooney, despite our occasional misunderstandings. But here is the problem: how can I guarantee that the reality I wake him to will be any less horrifying than the dream world he is trapped in now, asleep?

Winter makes itself known. The toilets overflow all at once, a blockage caused by a pipe not buried deep enough, a cold more penetrating than thought possible in the optimistic days when this place was built. The result is a reek which puts everyone in a foul humor, not least the guards who must escort us to a group of Porta Potties dumped haphazardly in the yard. Defecating is an act not easily performed in shackles. You have to be a Houdini to wipe yourself with any kind of effectiveness. Yet being released is at the individual guard's discretion.

"You're not going to make a mess, are you, Harms?"

"No, sir."

A lock being sprung, the most visceral sound known to modern man.

"Ankles?" I risk, about to shuffle into the plastic box.

"Hell, no."

I do not take it personally. This particular guard, Harris, is fat, and would have to bend over.

The interior is repulsive even by the low standards we have set. I shiver, trying to squeeze out a coil, feeling my life drop away.

After a while, Harris bangs on the side.

"Doing my best, sir."

Even if he had released me, what difference would it make? The tentative, hesitating step leg-irons demand has become second nature. Should this entire collection of buildings suddenly fall to the ground, leaving me alone unscathed, should the shackles themselves turn brittle and crack, I would no doubt continue my routine, pushing open the wide, crash-bar doors, crossing the yard with my maddeningly timid gait, as if nothing had changed.

Back in the cell, I rub where the freezing metal has left marks. I imagine there are similar welts on my brain, punishment for attempts to move too boldly from thought to thought. The pervasive cold has somewhat lessened the din of the place, though from the row above I hear a piece of metal being dragged relentlessly across the bars. Nostalgia for music maybe. Or a sadistic wish to drive us all insane.

Unlike normal prisoners, we are not permitted work. Instead we spend most of the day and all night in our cells. The resulting boredom is worse punishment than could be inflicted by any medieval torture device. To stare and know there will be no change in what you are staring at, that this brick or steel bar is waiting you out, will be here long after you are gone; to count, to feel, every heartbeat, its irretrievable beginning, middle, and end, is a bleak existence. There is the mind, of course. You can ransack it for memories, you can heave the tired apparatus into motion and try cooking up a fantasy or two, but after a very short time these lose their appeal. That is when the real thinking starts. What you called "thought" before was just play, a consciousness amusing itself when it had no news from outside to keep it busy. Now you are thrown back upon a way of being far more primitive.

I do not know who I am anymore. When I arrived, I had a very strong sense of self, but the borders have blurred. Perhaps, as Cooney hinted, it is compensation for my physical world being so circumscribed. If I am penned in by walls, counts, and curfews, my spirit takes up the slack, roams where flesh and blood cannot. Molecules of awareness waft out through the bars and mingle with those of others. There is a vast cloud of frustration choking the hallways, the maze-like ceilings, all the interstices of this unwieldy man-made organism. It is not, however, some mystical union with the Godhead. What I feel is the rage of a

million pent-up desires. My skin crawls with sins festering inside a multitude of living corpses. We are bad,
singly and collectively, yet all that perversity, that darkness, squeezed together, communing, has a warmth to
it. Whether I like it or not, these men are my brothers.

"Trays," a voice calls, pushing a trolley loaded with
everyone's customized dosage.

It is Mr. Mitra, the administrator.

"Where's Lanza?"

"Sergeant Lanza is sick. Flu."

"What about the other guards?"

"I am dispensing medication today."

"So I see."

Mr. Mitra handles the everyday running of the facility. He is one of those super-smart immigrants permanently stuck in a subordinate position even though he
knows more than anyone else. Back home in Bombay,
or wherever he is from, he would probably be an engi-
neer. He is the only suit-and-tie worker who dares
come into the Residential Wing as it is euphemistically
called. Thick, black-framed glasses indicate his mix of
intelligence and myopia.

"620003," he reads. "Harms, Ethan."

They are still called trays from a previous system.
In reality, we are given disposable cups, our name
written on the side, each with a specific assortment of
colors, shapes, and sizes jumbled at the bottom. The
treat, the incentive for taking them, is a pint of Tropicana Orange Juice. I glance at my potpourri. Over the
years, it has grown to resemble a garish sore.

"How was your holiday, Mr. Mitra?"

"My what?"

"Christmas. What did you do?"

He stares, surprised I am capable of grasping the fact that he has a life.

"My family and I attended church."

"You're Christian?"

"Of course."

"You know it's all based on pagan ritual, don't you? He's the sacrificial king."

I often wonder how much of my mood is attributable to medication. My pills are relatively straightforward. I do not suffer from schizophrenia and so am not burdened by the side effects of the antipsychotics. I am subject to mania, indeed I am only myself when enjoying at least a touch of that condition. Anything more than a touch, however, results in inappropriate behavior. When excited I take things too seriously, as if they existed, as if they mattered. So I am stomped on hard by various sedatives which bring with them their own heinous message: that the world is Satan's fart, that any movement, mental or physical, requires displacing every other atom in the universe and is therefore hardly worth the effort. It is a cycle, my mood, and the pills are not very sophisticated in keeping up with it. I have tried explaining to Mbaéré that if I was allowed to self-administer I could do a better job. I could strike that delicate balance between wishing to rocket out of my socks and resembling a puddle of protoplasm on the floor. He regards this request as proof of my instability and doles out the recommended dosage regardless of whatever my chemical levels may be that day.

"Who is the sacrificial king?" Mitra frowns.

"Jesus. In primitive cultures they used to chop Him up and sprinkle His blood on the fields. Kind of like fertilizer, if you think about it. Maybe they weren't so primitive after all."

"We are Baptists."

"It's all pre-Christian. That's what I'm trying to tell you. Here, the time we live in now, is Before."

He nods to the cup.

"If you would please take your medication. I have many more to do."

"Of course that's Easter," I amend. "The sacrifice of the king. I'm getting ahead of myself. Christmas is all about hope. Renewal. In the depths of winter, the promise of life. But Jesus? I don't know about Him."

This disturbs Mr. Mitra. He rubs his eyes. Although he is distracted for only a moment, I seize the opportunity and stuff the pills down the front of my pants.

"God's only Son," he corrects.

I take a big swallow, pretending to wash down the combined load all at once.

"Jesus Christ. Our Lord and Savior. He is not a king in some myth."

He checks the cup, to make sure it is empty.

"He was sent here to save us from death."

"That's been kind of an uphill battle, wouldn't you say? What's the score so far? About a trillion-seventy-five to zero?"

"It appears Sergeant Lanza will be out for quite some while. Perhaps we can continue this conversation next time."

"I look forward to that."

"Trays," he calls, trundling on.

I shake the pills out of my pant leg and grind them into the floor. I do not know what I am doing, a sure sign it is worthwhile. I would never have risked this with Lanza or one of the other guards. My heel seeks out each one, each brightly colored petal of hell, and tries eradicating its very existence. How many years now have I been subjected to this chemical poisoning and willingly acquiesced, believing what they told me, that it would make me more rational, that it would dull the urges that got me sent here in the first place, that it would enable me, for the first time ever, to truly understand what it is like to be a human being? I grind these very concepts into the cement, then spit to darken any last vestige of the aesthetically objectionable colors.

Like a Walt Disney cartoon, a Day-Glo palette for life well-lived.

Flu has decimated the staff. Mitra is a nice guy, not a compliment in this part of the world. He is easy to distract.

A long-sleeping creature twitches behind my eyes.

4.

Newcomers provide material for all sorts of rumor and speculation. Mostly, though, what goes through the yard when a fresh set of features appears is lust. We are tired of each other's repulsive appearance. Like the wires and pipes, the cells and floors, our faces have been degraded to an institutional sameness. So when a stranger arrives still bearing the faint bloom of having once been alive we all fall in love. Those who want to do violence dream of that. Those who express themselves pornographically narrow their gaze in a different way. Those who perceive beauty as a threat, a rebuke to the death-in-life they have chosen to worship, stare warily. But all our hearts race. Everyone is momentarily transformed. It is as if one of those planes which fly lazily overhead made an emergency landing and a young aviator stepped out. Certainly that is the case today. Littlejohn, the object of everyone's attention, is remarkably shy and youthful. He paces the perimeter, a lost child, head down, newly issued shoes kicking at the narrow margin of dirt.

"Super Glue?"

"That's how they found them. He had stuck their mouths shut."

"You could still breathe through your nose."

"Only a little bit."

"Only if he let you. Only if he didn't pinch it off."

"But how did he get them to stay still until it set?"

That is the mystery. He does not have the physique to overpower. He must have relied on charm. The men were bigger. Older.

"Maybe he hypnotized them."

None of us know anything. It is a game of Telephone, becoming wilder and more embellished with each telling. He turns, revealing a handsome face, square jaw, regular features, all unmarked, like a male model. We do not breathe. He has glued our lips shut as well.

I am sitting next to Crow, who smells particularly bad this afternoon. His pants are stiff. To try and escape this pull of unwilling attraction, I move closer, entering the soap bubble of silence. A brief acknowledgment passes over his vacant gaze, or so I imagine.

I am worried about my mother, I transmit.

It is a psychic message. We are touching all along one side.

She's getting older. Not so much in her age but in her mind. Some of the things she writes in her last letter don't make sense. I mean, they do to me but only because I know the direction her thoughts go in. And her handwriting, there's something off about it. I can't say exactly what. It tastes different.

Around us, men speak but no sound comes out.

One of the worst things about a closed environment is that you cannot reveal anything without it becoming public knowledge. Paradoxically, the urge to confide under such circumstances grows unbearably intense. You see people whispering to walls, shouting incoherently at empty skies. Anything to get a piece of information *out* while not having it come back to damage them. But I can talk to Crow. It is like dropping news down a well.

I'm not just her son. We grew up together. She was young when she had me. So we're kind of like best friends. Not that I really understand friendship. Is it just the state that exists before betrayal?

There is the notion of a frown on Crow's face, indistinguishable really from his otherwise stoic features.

I'd like to see her. Check up on her. She could come visit. She's my designated next of kin. But she never showed much interest.

Littlejohn wanders too close to the forbidden section of wall where massive doors for oversized deliveries sit bolted shut. The tower guard yells through a bullhorn. Why he always yells when his voice is already electronically amplified I will never know. Free people's actions are inexplicable.

It's just that, without me there, I'm worried she'll go into some kind of spiral. At first she seemed to be getting along OK, but now . . . People take advantage of her. She's very vulnerable. She doesn't appear that way from the outside, but . . . The question is, what can I do? Would I even be such a help if I could magically appear by her side? What the hell good did you do before, when you actually were there? Of course some would say it's the other way around. That she was no help to you.

Language is collapsing. I do not know whom I address, the catatonic Injun whose stink is becoming my own or the me who only comes into existence intermittently, when I can filter out the noise, the chatter, the mind-destroying substitute that passes for conversation here and so gauge accurately just how rudimentary my own mental faculties have become.

She's the only mother I got, I conclude.

If you call that a conclusion.

Littlejohn approaches. He has blue eyes and sandy hair. He makes the mistake of settling down on the seemingly empty two-thirds of Stanley's bench.

There is a mass intake of breath, an orgy of anticipation. Sad to say, but we live for moments like this.

Stanley's body begins its slow change. He is not strong looking. He appears to be boneless. There is a rubbery sameness to his limbs, to his trunk, even to his head, as if he emerged from a mold rather than developed organically. When aroused, this undifferentiated mass swells all at once, like a penis. Even the other telltale sign bears out that comparison, a thick trickle of saliva dripping from the corner of his mouth.

"Someone sitting here?" Littlejohn frowns, way too late.

Stanley is a surprisingly conventional fighter. He punches. That is all he does. With his thumbs, of course, and between the legs a few times, but he never chokes or kicks or gouges. If his opponent falls, he waits. He obeys a code, albeit an inscrutable one, allowing the man to get up on at least one knee before walloping him again. All this time his face has a friendly, eager, dog-like expression. The others form a circle, yelling, urging Littlejohn on, not because they favor him but because they want more of a contest than the usual one-sided beatdown. The guards watch. They have no great motivation to intervene. Stanley is doing their job for them, introducing Littlejohn to our hierarchy. Crow and I remain, staring at emptied blacktop.

I knew this priest, I resume. He used to make rubbings of old gravestones. There was a cemetery out back of the church. He would rub chalk over blank sheets of newsprint to get a facsimile of some long-deceased townsperson's inscription. I don't know why he did it. There were no fancy designs or famous names. I don't know what happened to the pages either. I never saw them framed or hung on a wall.

The crowd gives a fireworks-display gasp of appreciation as Stanley lands a particularly devastating blow. Those pristine features are unmarked no longer. Now when Littlejohn looks in the metal over the sinks he will have the same experience as the rest of us, confronting his twisted visage.

I remember how the letters would magically appear when Father Bryan was rubbing away. Like he was raising the dead.

The guards finally wade in, swinging their sticks.

They line us up for an early count. Because everyone was in a circle I do not get to insert myself where I usually do. Whom you end up next to, in any situation, is of prime importance here. There is an art to the seemingly random movement of a scattered group transforming itself into a straight line. I am forced to fall in at the end, next to Littlejohn. Freshly beaten, he has not yet found his place. His angelic face is somewhat worse for the wear. Not so bad as it will be, though, once the swelling sets in. He stands at a tilt, one testicle crushed.

"It's OK," I murmur, as they go down the row. "It's not personal with Stanley."

He does not seem to hear. He is busy surreptitiously examining his cheek, seeking out the bone, feeling if it is still intact.

"He likes to put on a show. You stay away from him and it's not like he'll come looking for you. You got to understand, there's spheres of influence here. You just wandered into his by accident."

He looks over. His eyes, even the one that is going to close up in a few hours, have a remarkable depthlessness to them. They are highway reflectors. Your own concern gives them life. Otherwise they are dead.

"—name's Ethan."

"Fuck you," he hisses, as the guard comes up.

THERE'S WEATHER and there's weather. With so little opportunity to experience the turning of the seasons, we create our own atmospherics, a "winter within," bringing its own sense of hibernation, of storing up.

Outwardly our routine remains the same, but with a ghost-like drift. Part of us is elsewhere, dreaming in its cave, preparing for an equally self-constructed spring, one of feeling, again with no outward sign.

I find myself staring in an unfocused, uninquiring way. The muscles that control the movements of my eyes go slack. I do not see anything, not even a blur. If spoken to, I make no distinction between the real and the imagined. The wall between fact and reverie vanishes.

How much longer until death? That is the only remaining question. The rest is a veneer we labor to maintain so as not to spend all our waking hours brooding over this last unknown.

A rat appears. Conditions drive them in. I am not as squeamish as some. Rats don't bother you if you leave them be, though the way they slip through tiny spaces, squeezing to nothing without visible effort, resuming their normal dimensions on the other side, is unnerving.

"Won't find much here," I warn, watching him hug the wall and sniff for food.

With guards, they have much worse relations. Rats are not as obedient as prisoners. They are roaming evil. Most officers curse when they see one. Some even run away. It is one of the main complaints made by their union, I am told, "rodent infestation," right up there with the cancer cluster we supposedly host.

"Shoo," I say idly.

It is nibbling air, so far as I can tell, a crumb at best, or maybe some microscopic insect.

There are unexplained drafts. For a facility supposed to be impenetrable, whose very design is based on limiting entrance and egress, you would think wind would not have such an easy time blasting down passageways, taking up residence in specific cells, raising dust devils of grit.

If my soul were taken now, I do not think it would be sufficiently cleansed to merit salvation. But if I was found wanting, then death might pass unnoticed, appear as an inconvenience, a transfer from one section of the complex to another. Hell, assuming it exists, would still be confinement and pain, remorse and suffering. The only change will be one of degree. I cannot imagine the food being any worse. If, however, some honest intention of repentance is recognized, if I am given conditional entrée to a higher level of being, then death would indeed be as advertised. I try imagining the shock, torn loose from every familiar mooring, the terror of rebirth, the agony of seeing—with a mercilessly accurate retrospection I now lack—transgressions I committed. Heaven, though by definition *good*, would take some getting used to.

Would it be worth it?

With a quick movement, I catch the rat, dangle it by the tail. It contorts, tries to shinny up its own self and bite. I let it drop just in time, hear its teeth click on the way down. They do not land like cats, they become a ball, rolling along, perhaps to evade hawks, before suddenly regaining traction and scooting off.

Such are the straits boredom reduces one to.

And so another day is clubbed to insensibility.

Showering takes on a great significance. Some cower from the hot water as if it will wash away their essential nature. Others hog, trying to take more than their allotted forty seconds of blissful relief. Closing your eyes and thrusting your face into the steam, you can actually pretend you are not here. It is one of the few experiences the same inside as out. The guard in charge keeps a rhythmic tap with his stick, and woe to him who does not move along. Retribution comes not from the authorities but the man standing behind, waiting.

There is also the naked aspect. All of us cling to what little privacy remains, but here the last shred is ripped away. We shy, with our eyes and with our movements, like lambs in a fold. Which makes Eldridge's death all the more disturbing.

"He just sat down."

"In the shower?"

"On the tiles. I told him, 'You shouldn't do that. There's all kinds of infection there.' People get athlete's foot, toenail fungus. I can't even imagine what happens if you set your naked butt by the drain like that. Plus, of course, it screws up the rotation. We have to be in and out in twenty minutes. All of us. That's how much hot water there is."

"So you spoke to him?"

"He had a tattoo. I'd never noticed before. Real faded. All this hair growing through it."

"A tattoo of what?"

I frown.

"I don't see what relevance that would have to your doctoral thesis. Before you acted like personal information was—"

"Obviously it's important to you, what you're telling me, and your psychology is germane to my study."

"Plus you're curious."

"All right, I'm curious."

"Even though it's unprofessional?"

Since our initial encounters, I have learned how to look back at her. There is a hood that comes down, further inside, a second eyelid I use to regulate things, to protect me from feeling overly exposed. I sense others employ this mechanism without even being aware. For me, it is still a challenge.

"When did you realize he was gone?"

"He was just sitting there."

I meditate on how not to pull the wrist shackles. I recognize it as a sign that I am in danger of having an attack. People dismiss things as mere symptoms, but I believe that if you address the so-called symptoms nine times out of ten the problem will take care of itself. Now when I have the urge to yank on the steel rings I talk my hands down, soothe them as one would a pair of savage beasts. Of course if they are independent entities I have no idea what that makes the rest of me. A different creature. Not-my-hands, for starters.

"It sounds awful," she says.

"What? Him dying? He murdered an entire family with a machete."

"That's awful too."

"How come you never talked to him? He could have told you about aspects of the pathological mind."

"His profile didn't fit the parameters. He had aged out."

She has changed as well. She appears more human, more worn and chipped around the edges, than when I first met her. She is not dressed with as much formality, in jeans now, sneakers, and a red-checked lumberman's shirt. Her hair is still pulled back, but I can see her neck and make out the shape of her shoulders. Her nails are no longer painted, or rather they are, but painted clear. They still glow.

"Count your breaths."

"What?"

"You're panting."

"I'm trying to stop my hands from—"

"You're upset about your friend dying."

"He wasn't my friend."

"Count your breaths. One for inhale, two for exhale, three for inhale, and so on. Go ahead. Try. It's simple."

Even though it seems silly, I breathe, keeping track in my head. She has her notebook out. I never know when she is going to write. Sometimes I will say the most innocuous thing and she will scribble furiously. Other times, I come out with a weighty pronouncement and she looks right through me, like I am the clear polish on those nails.

"Twenty-five . . ." I haul in the sweet scent she has brought with her, the air of forests and streams, of car exhaust and highway convenience stores, all of it delicious. "Twenty-six . . ." Blow it out in a solid, concentrated shaft.

"There." She leans forward, puts her palms over my clasped hands. They are no longer aspiring to sever themselves from the rest of me. "What were you thinking about, these last few minutes?"

"Nothing."

"That's mindfulness."

It is the first time we have touched. One of my fingers, a rogue, a joker, an explorer, frees itself from the others and comes to rest on the soft skin of her knuckle.

I wait for her to scream.

"Try doing that five minutes a day."

"What happens then?"

"Nothing. Just do it five minutes a day. That's more than most people are truly aware."

"I couldn't save him."

"Who?"

"Eldridge." I feel I have to offer something in exchange for what she has given me. It is strange, telling the truth. I have trouble fitting my mouth around the words. "I wanted to save him. I wanted him to feel remorse."

"That's good, Ethan. That's a positive impulse. Why do you sound so guilty, saying it out loud?"

"Not my concern really. Besides, who am I to be giving advice?"

She takes her hand away.

"How old are you?" I ask.

"There's another personal question."

"I thought we were past that."

"I don't want this to become something it's not."

"You get to ask all sorts of personal questions."

"They're not personal *to me*."

The hell they aren't, I frown, but say out loud:

"I could draw it, if you want. The tattoo you were so interested in. The one on Eldridge's shoulder."

I indicate the splayed-open notebook. She pushes it toward me. I manage to pick up the pen and sketch the outline of a butterfly. It does not emerge the way I intend. I do not mean for it to appear so disgustingly sexual.

"You're a lefty."

"Finally something about me you didn't already know."

The hair. It is the hair growing through the wings. And the skin underneath. An old man's rough hide. Cooling now. Slack.

"What did you do for Christmas?" I resume.

"Nice try."

"I'm serious."

"I'd like to keep the focus on you, if that's all right."

"Sure." I push back the notebook. "Focus on me all you want. Right now the number one thing on my pathological mind is, 'What did Dr. Roberta Bush do for Christmas?' "

She turns the picture around and starts writing underneath it.

"Hang up a stocking?"

From the way she does not answer, I know it is true.

"One stocking, all alone? Why is that such a sad sight? Because socks come in pairs, I suppose. So when we see just one, it implies loss."

"This is very well drawn. Did you take lessons?"

"What? In butterflies?"

"Art."

"I never took a lesson my entire life. In anything."

"I'm not surprised."

"What's that supposed to mean?"

"You're a classic autodidact."

"Sounds like an insult."

"It's not. An autodidact is just someone who's self-taught."

"I know what the word means."

She is still writing. She fills the entire page.

"It's not uncommon for people of your type. You have extensive, idiosyncratic knowledge in certain subjects and correspondingly vast ignorance of others, in those that don't interest you, or that make you feel threatened."

"Never went past the eleventh grade."

"That's a shame." ·

"Not really. Look at you. Your learning's all homogenized. Predigested. It's based on people telling you things. Lies mostly. Or half-truths. What I know, I know from having made the effort to find out."

I imagine my hand exploring the interior of her lone stocking, the one she salvaged from childhood that now hangs on a doorknob or over the TV. It is grotesquely oversized. My arm goes up all the way to the elbow. I spread my fingers. She tenses as if I was inside her.

"So what'd you get?" I ask. "What did Santa bring?"

She closes the book and puts away the pen. Because she has left all her devices behind, neither of us has the time, yet she always seems to know exactly when the session is over.

"I'd like you to draw more, Ethan. Would you do that for me?"

"Draw what?"

"Whatever you want."

There is always a helpless feeling when she leaves, as if I have failed, as if I could have made her stay forever by saying the right thing.

"I can't draw."

"I'll arrange to have materials sent to you. I don't think the authorities would mind."

"That's not what I meant. I can't—"

She is already up. I try to rise with her, a reflex action despite years of painful experience. Always get up when a lady enters or leaves the room.

"I'm sorry if I offended you. I just wanted to know what gifts you got for Christmas. That's all."

"I'm not offended, Ethan. I'm . . ."

She does not complete the sentence. She goes. People are always leaving. Outsiders. They have no idea what a luxury it is, to choose when an encounter is over. Over for them. For me, stuck here, encounters never really stop. They overlay each other and deepen.

Sometimes it takes the guard fifteen minutes to remember I am still here, to come in and unshackle me. I sniff the air where she sat, trying to gather up whatever has been left behind, trying to reconstitute her from sensory experience alone.

5.

Dear Mother,

It is strange to confront an envelope I have already sent. I feel the same anticipation as if it was from a stranger, which I suppose it is. A previous me.

Merry Christmas! What are you doing for the holiday? Do you remember the time we tried to make a tree out of a mop? I do not think green food coloring has ever been used to a more odd purpose. Why did you even have that box of food dye in the cupboard? Not to make cupcakes, surely. Was it left by the family who lived there before us? So much seemed to have been. I used to wonder about them, try to piece together what they were like by the furniture and knickknacks they left behind. Green food coloring. Maybe they were Irish?!

I shake my head at the tone. Eager to please. Always trying to amuse. I imagine her holding the flimsy prison issue paper with distaste, noting the contrast with the substantial stationery she uses, our only physical link over the years.

I am so sorry you were once again not able to make the journey. I would have liked to sit across from you and share memories of the great times we had, how you would come home and I would hear about your "day" before bringing you the silly excuse for dinner I had prepared.

Christmas here was a rather disappointing affair. We were served a semi-frozen piece of meat wrapped in soggy dough. Only after poking it several times did I realize it was supposed to be Beef Wellington! I suppose Warden, a kind man [all correspondence is read by the authorities before being sent out] *was trying to give us a treat. Several residents expressed their displeasure by using it to decorate the walls. They were disciplined. Hardly an example of peace on earth and good will toward men!*

You mention Star Market in your last. Do you remember the time I attempted to make Cheese Danish because the bakery you used to go to had closed? I found a recipe and snuck off to Star Market, buying all the ingredients on the sly. What a surprise I hoped to give you! I will never forget the look on your face when we opened the oven to confront a sea of melted, burning butter! You were angry at the time, but you must admit the aroma it left was lovely. It must have lingered in the kitchen for several years. I can still smell it if I close my eyes.

The RETURN TO SENDER mark across the address is fresh and clean. I would have thought it a faded, cracked, rubber stamp wielded with reluctance, not so new and brash-looking a dismissal.

Several things you said in your last letter gave me cause for concern. Were you pulling my leg? I do not think the "world" is quite as vibrant as you make it out to be. Those stares you claim to feel, for example. Perhaps they are looks of admiration, if not downright envy! Remember, you are a beautiful woman.

I note the gap, the small space of hesitation where I considered writing "still," as in "still a beautiful woman" before rejecting the idea.

The important thing is to take care of yourself and not let these people's "bad energy," as you call it, dampen your spirits. Are you still trying to eat three meals a day? Do not discount the healthful effects of such a simple achievement. Remember, I am counting on you. You are my lifeline.

Back home, I did not have a room, as such. The book shelf that comprised the wall of the alcove where I slept was another legacy from the previous tenants. They must have left in a hurry, or perhaps did not have money for movers. Their absence was as much a mystery as our presence. I had vague memories of a time before, but those were mixed with make-believe and television cartoons. Father, for example, existed as two confused conflicting references. There was "your father," a man we had once lived with, who had held me, though not lovingly or for long, but there was also "your *father*," a shadowy figure, less human, less defined, more like fate or bad luck or an amalgam of all that had happened to Mother since my birth. "Your *father*" was what landed us in these rundown cramped rooms cluttered with some other family's leavings. He was the malevolence that had left Mother in such an untenable position, forcing her to balance two competing if not contradictory elements: her wish to live and my mute demand for all her love.

That is where books came in. In light of her refusal
to give me even the basic facts of our hand-to-mouth
existence, its causes or any sense of where it might
lead, I got the curious notion I could read my way out,
devouring the contents of the wall that kept me from
the other side of the living room, where Mother's stifled laughs became sobs, where men I was never introduced to cleared their throats.

At first I chose randomly, by the color of the spine
or the location. The shelf had no backing. It was meant
to be up against something. It swayed in the night air.
When I removed a book, I created a chink in the otherwise solid barrier. It is unclear to me if I actually read,
at the start. More likely I mimicked the act, approaching the problem externally, staring at each page for
a set amount of time and then turning it, pretending
I had gleaned knowledge—which I had, not via the
text but through the hole I could now see through.
I kept the books on the floor by my mattress. Later,
when Mother came back, I pressed my nose up to
the musty tomes and made out through dim light . . .
nothing really. Rarely was anything going on in the
narrow slit my "reading" afforded me. But I could
hear and be more fully with them, just by virtue of
actively eavesdropping. Once she did happen to step
into my severely restricted field of vision. There was a
night-light plugged into a baseboard outlet, so I could
find my way to the bathroom or go to the kitchen for
a glass of water. In its ghostly rays an almost unrecognizable woman appeared. She was younger, more alive
than the wearied, defeated scold I knew. She was also
quite clearly in the throes of something. I crouched by
my keyhole and saw a second, nearly invisible figure

burrowing into that mysterious region between neck and shoulder. I could not see him. He was more a demon, a narrow tapering snout butchering her with feeling. He found a weak spot and exploited it. She tried to get away but her actions were self-defeating, drawing him deeper in. There were hands. I could not see them from my vantage point but there must have been hands, lower down, steel restraints denying any possibility of escape. She gave a low, keening cry. Then everything stopped. A line had been crossed. The man cleared his throat. They disappeared from the makeshift stage. The bedroom door opened and closed, closed decisively, introducing me to a new world of loneliness.

All from reading, my mind convinced its naive charge.

I had a flashlight as well. I was afraid of the dark. I took down another book, got under the covers and sealed them tight, creating a small, flimsy tent. I trained the yellow beam and began moving my lips in earnest.

They were cookbooks, I realize now. At the time, I made no distinction. All I knew was that by expanding the hole in the wall, brick by brick, I was increasing the chances I would find what was on the other side. The only way to truly see was to read each volume as it came down. By chance or unconscious determination, I seized upon an area containing large picture volumes with photos of luminous soups and browned, juicy roasts. Summer salads rose up like forests. One chocolate cake, a geometrically precise wedge cut out, flaunted its layers and icing and fantastic decorations. I pored over that composition. It was a church from some far more fortunate planet than the one I was stranded on. The specially treated paper that received high gloss reproductions had a peculiar aroma. I shone my flashlight, movable bull's-eye, and worked my way through the recipes as if they were fairy tales or a hero's adventures.

If you are dead, surely I would have been notified. You are my designated next of kin, as I am yours. If I had died they would have notified you. Then you would finally come, to collect my remains, maybe have them interred in the old cemetery in back of Holy Spirit, although recently I heard— not to gossip—some rather disturbing news about Father Bryan. He has long since been reassigned, I assume. But the point is, I am not dead and neither are you! So why have you moved without telling me?

I pause, paper in hand, realizing that none of this is taking place. I am amending a letter that has never been delivered. Were I to sniff it, lick it, tear it with my teeth, it would only give back the poisons of its origin. I am not even holding a pencil. I glare accusingly at my fingers and remember certain things they did, of their own volition, although they would contend they were obeying orders.

"World of hurt! World of hurt!" someone promises, continuing a petty feud across acres of locked space. He repeats it until it becomes pure sound, a chant: "Worldofhurt worldofhurt . . ."

Someone else is banging his head against a non-functioning toilet bowl, producing a specific note: bone on porcelain.

I HAVE never been to this wing of the facility before. It is near the outside gate, an area to which prisoners

are not normally permitted access. Walking the hallway "loose," without ankle or wrist restraints, I try not
to gape at the simplest things: a poster commemorat-
ing some sort of event, a table set against the wall on
which sit a coffeemaker, Styrofoam cups, a small metal
bucket containing packets of sugar. My digestion reacts
as a starving tiger's would at the sight of gazelle. The
guard, one I do not know, he does not work the main
building, stops me before a door.

After a moment, seeing I am not used to taking the
initiative, he opens it for me.

At first I am disappointed. It is merely a collection
of chairs grouped around a clear plastic cube scattered
with magazines. A plant grows in one corner, a small
creeping vine. I do not see how it survives. There is no
window. A woman, older, distracted, has a telephone
hunched between her shoulder and ear. The guard
points to a chair. When I am seated, I see another door,
with a placard on it, and realize this is a waiting room,
an outer office. Only then do I understand where I
have been summoned to.

"Ethan." Warden smiles, not very convincingly. "So
glad you could join us."

This time I am not asked to sit. There is a chair
opposite the desk but it is occupied by a man clearly
from some world other than the Federal Bureau of
Prisons. He wears a thick, colorful sweater. It is the
shape of a jacket, but knitted, with geometric patterns
running through the wool. His wire-rimmed glasses,
blue jeans, and expensive cowboy boots would not last
ten seconds in the yard.

"This is Harms," Warden continues.

Never healthy-looking, Warden seems to have declined since I last saw him. There is a touch of gray, not so much in his hair as in his pallor. He is, as I said, relatively young, but his hands are restless and his gaze hollow. He reminds me of fruit you buy that never ripens, that remains stone hard on the counter until rot sets in.

By contrast, the newcomer is unsettlingly alive. He leans forward, all cuddly in his sweater-jacket.

"He seems a little light for the job."

"Ethan is very intelligent."

"That's what I mean."

I am not even attempting to understand what they are talking about. The sensory overload here is profound. So much is wood, the desk, the frames of the family photos, the paneling on the walls. I have not consciously missed luxurious appointments during my time of incarceration but to be suddenly surrounded by stains and grains, not to mention deep carpeting and strong unsullied light coming from a freshly washed window, makes it clear just how deeply and how long I have been deprived. I blink back tears, not out of emotion but to cleanse my pupils so I can more accurately register the wonders.

"What do you think, Ethan?" Warden goes on. "We have a job for you, but we wouldn't want you to over-analyze it."

The man stares as if I am on display. We have not been introduced, nor will we be, I can tell.

"Harms is usually more articulate."

"The box."

Warden smiles as if to say, See?

It is a large cardboard box resting on his desk. The top has already been opened.

"How did you know it was for you?"

I do not answer. Rather, after his permission-giving nod, I reach in and carefully lift out sheets of heavy paper, the kind with ragged edges like cloth. There are also sticks of charcoal in various shapes and sizes.

"You made quite an impression on the PhD candidate. She sent these after her last visit. She seems to feel they could be therapeutic."

"*Materials*," I dredge up the word.

"Yes. Drawing materials. Do you draw, Ethan?"

"No."

"Thank god for that. I think we've encouraged enough self-expression around here. For one lawsuit, at least."

They are not items you would buy at the stationery aisle of a drugstore but the real thing, what artists use. I have never encountered such quality before, but I can tell. I hold the rods of charcoal as I would ingots of gold.

"I can keep them?"

"Of course you can."

"I can take them back to my cell?"

"I don't see why not."

He looks past me to the unnamed visitor.

"Ethan," Sweater Man begins, forming a tent with his fingertips, "does Mr. Cooney ever talk about his past?"

"Who?"

"Raymond Cooney. Your cellmate."

"He's not my cellmate."

"I was under the impression you and Mr. Cooney shared a cell."

I appeal to Warden.

"All prisoners are kept in individual units. Considering their tendency to become active it was thought best not for them to have too much common contact."

"Locusts," I elaborate.

"So technically there are no cellmates, though Harms's and Cooney's cells have been across from each other for over two years."

"The way when you crowd grasshoppers together they mutate, undergo a change."

"I'm interested in any or all comments Mr. Cooney may have made to you about his crimes," the man tries again.

" —become spotted and voracious. Locusts."

"Just tell him what he wants to know, Ethan."

"What crimes?"

I clutch the mound of paper to my chest as if it could protect me.

"I'm particularly interested in his victims. Has he ever talked about them individually?"

"His brides."

"What?"

"That's what he calls them. His brides. Like he was some kind of serial Mormon. Haven't you read his book? Everyone else has. All about the 'epiphany' he experienced exploring 'the dark side of the American soul?' "

"I'm familiar with his book, yes."

"What's galling is he can't even spell the word epiphany much less experience one. He doesn't have the spiritual equipment to—"

"I'm not interested in his religion. I'm interested in any additional victims he may not have yet admitted killing. One victim in particular. A body that may still be out there."

"Why would he do that? I mean, why would he hold something like that back? He's not shy."

Warden shakes his head.

"This is exactly what my friend here was worried about. That you would ask your own questions instead of answering ours."

"People say that you are the only person Mr. Cooney opens up to. That you and he share a kind of intimacy."

"The hell we do."

"There's nothing wrong with being intimate. I mean, there is," Warden hastily amends. "There can be."

He gets lost for a moment in some private unsavory thought.

"Let's wrap this up, shall we?" He talks exclusively to Sweater Man, staring through me. "The longer he's here the more talk there's going to be."

"You think I'd sell out Cooney for a bunch of art supplies?"

"No one's asking you to violate a confidence, Ethan. All we're interested in is information. The truth."

"Truth!"

I try spitting the word, but it is one of those concepts you can never truly free yourself of.

"There may be an additional woman," Sweater Man says. "In the ground. She deserves to be properly cared for, and mourned."

"She's mourned."

I think of Cooney's restless, tortured sleep.

"Not if her people don't know for certain that she's dead. Not if they haven't seen her body."

"Bodies aren't dead."

I regret the words as soon as they pass my lips. It is private knowledge I am letting them in on, knowledge which, for these two clowns, would be unearned. Luckily they are too dense to understand. They let it fly by their ears rather than deal with its disturbing implications. So much for truth.

"Get Cooney to talk," Warden summarizes. "There's a seventeenth victim, one not mentioned in the book. Find out where she is."

"She have a name?"

"She does have a name," Sweater Man says.

"It's very important to me personally, Ethan." Warden looks me over. The desk is too wide for him to reach across, but his sad eyes produce the same effect. They grope various parts of my body, trying to get closer, trying to feel what I feel. "Some of what Cooney is asking to see in these Motions of Discovery could put me in an awkward position."

He pushes the box, which contains still more paper, until it almost tips over the edge. I catch it and stuff everything back in.

"The materials will be an excuse to justify your visit."

"Always taking care of me, huh?"

"I am, Ethan. I have your best interests at heart. Make sure people see them. I don't want them to get the wrong idea."

"It would help if I knew her name."

"You have to find that out from him," Sweater Man says. "That's how we'll know you're not bullshitting us."

"Ethan doesn't bullshit," Warden says sadly. "He can't. That's one of the reasons he's here."

The gap between dinner and breakfast is always the worst. By our thirteenth straight hour of confinement there is a continuous roar.

"Set it on fire!" someone suggests.

Another extends the thought to its logical conclusion:

"Burn the motherfucking motherfucker to the motherfucking ground!"

. . . with all us inside, I envision, sizzling like bacon.

That is your stomach talking, another part of me chastises, trying to erase the bacon reference from my consciousness before I stagger with hunger and longing.

Breakfast is a travesty, even in relation to the pitiful evening meal. Bacon and its holy brother sausage are nowhere in evidence. Once upon a time, I am told, it was hot, with eggs, albeit powdered, grits or potatoes, and a scrap of meat, though no one who remembers is willing to say exactly what type. Budget cuts have long since reduced this to a plastic basket, weirdly imitating wicker, in which are tossed a cellophane-wrapped biscuit, a wedge of processed milk product (nowhere on the minuscule lettering of the label do they dare use the word "cheese"), and a cup-sized container of water. Along with a napkin. The napkin I find particularly insulting. Such a dry, tasteless meal could never induce the need to wipe one's mouth. We are issued the basket, trooping along in a line, but not permitted to sit. This counts as our A.M. exercise. Once served, we return to our cells to eat and enjoy another four hours of forced contemplation.

"Don't you get hungry?" I ask Cooney, who is still locked in a standoff over some obscure interpretation of the rules. He has not gone—or has not been permitted to go—to breakfast in months. Unlike at dinnertime, they do not provide him with a substitute meal. Instead he meditates, remaining cross-legged on his bed.

"It's eating that makes you hungry," he answers, not bothering to open his eyes.

With the care of a safecracker I part the cellophane wrapper of the biscuit, insert the peeled wedge of "Cheez," reseal the assemblage as best I can, and jam it into the metal housing of the light fixture.

"Did you notice?" Cooney asks.

He is performing his intellectual calisthenics. His hands are set on top of his thighs, fingers making the "OK" sign.

"Notice what?"

"You didn't notice."

"You want me to ask for a second basket next time? I don't know if they'd give it to me but if I tell them it's for you . . ."

I take advantage of his detached state to examine him more closely. Why is he not wasting away? Are his boxed dinners ten times more nutritious than ours? He is sleek, a well-fed cat.

"The stars are out," he says, ignoring my offer.

"Stars? Open your eyes. It's eight o'clock."

"I'm talking about my book. There's been interest from various leading men."

"You got a favorite?"

"I'm more interested in the *actresses*." He pronounces the word carefully. "Seems like a great opportunity."

"You mean the victims?"

"You get yourself a bunch of young unknowns, the kind that come to Hollywood against all family advice, down to their last dollar, desperate, but so pretty."

"How long is each onscreen for?"

"It's not the quantity of the exposure, but the quality. How she performs under pressure. These can be very demanding roles."

". . . didn't notice what?" I frown, not wanting to go down that road. Not so early in the day. "What didn't I see out there?"

"Won't do any good for me to tell. You have to spot it on your own."

"All I see is more of the same."

"Because that's all you want to see. You don't see the machinations, the big picture, the forces at play."

"Why wouldn't I see those, if they existed?"

"Because then you'd have to act."

"Act? What kind of *act* can I perform in here?"

"Exactly."

He opens his eyes and yawns. Our conversation, up until now, was a dream. It no longer exists. Frowning, he sniffs in my direction. My eyes follow.

"Shit!"

I burn my fingers, retrieving the scorched packet of hot biscuit and liquefied whey.

"You ought to write a cookbook."

He watches me lick the concoction off the half-vaporized cellophane.

I am too intent on savoring every morsel to take offense.

"*Cooking for Life*. How's that for a title?"

"One hundred twenty-seven years," I correct.

"You missed your calling. You should have been a chef."

"A chef cooks for others."

I lap up the last bit.

"Trays," someone calls.

"Mr. Mitra!" Cooney greets him, my mouth being full. "Still doing other people's jobs for them?"

"Harms," he reads off a cup. "620003. What are you eating?"

"A kind of . . . melt," I manage to mumble, greedily eying the pint of Tropicana.

"They giving you time-and-a-half?" Cooney calls. "Should be some kind of hazard pay dealing with the likes of us. Don't you think?"

"I am a salaried employee," Mitra earnestly explains. "I do not receive an hourly wage."

"Just helping out, huh?"

He passes my cup through the slot and tries addressing me alone:

"I have been thinking about what you said."

I have no idea what he is talking about. All I can focus on is the prospect of a nice cool pull of orange juice. I toss back the cup's contents and raise the container to my lips.

"How's the evidence-gathering?" Cooney asks.

The pills travel to the hanging-down flap at the back of my throat, the uvula, and set off a gag reflex. I have gotten quite good at this over the past few weeks.

"Make sure you don't leave out any of those memos Warden sends. I know all the different addresses he uses."

I cough, then swallow. The medications undergo a weird trampolining effect. They are sucked up a secret chute.

"I do what Warden instructs me, Mr. Cooney. He is my superior. Not yourself."

"It's not Warden you should be obeying, but the court order. You violate that, it's your brown ass, not his. Did you know," he turns to me now, "that workplace e-mails are public documents? That the author of said e-mails has no legal expectation of privacy?"

"Are you all right?" Mitra frowns.

Mastering the spasm, I manage to choke down a few sips of juice. The pills are not in my throat or digestive tract. They are lodged in the nasal cavity behind my eyes, an empty space, a cavern or chamber where smells become thoughts.

"He's allergic."

"To what?"

"Salaried employees."

"I thought we could continue our discussion about Easter. I spoke to my pastor. He claims—"

"Whoa! Whoa! Can't you tell the man's in distress? Look at his face. It's beet red. Let him recover."

Mitra shrugs, disappointed.

"Another time perhaps."

I nod mutely. Once he is several cells down, I bury my face in the mattress and wretch. My head turns itself inside out from eyeballs to ears, expelling the intruders. After a time, they shoot from my nose, still intact, coated with phlegm and threads of blood.

"Coffee-colored bastard," Cooney grins.

I can barely speak my throat is so raw. I collect the evidence in my hand and scatter it over the malfunctioning toilet. The colors begin to dissolve.

"Why do you have it in for him?"

"He's the house nigger. Can't you tell? Does their dirty work for them. Hell, he *volunteers* to come in here. What kind of sadistic shit does that?"

"Just trying to help out."

"He's a spy, you idiot."

My body is still shaken from ridding itself of the pills. I sit down and hug my knees, rocking back and forth.

"What's it like?" Cooney asks.

I am surprised he is interested. He always takes his pills. It is the one part of the prison routine he seems eager to obey. I toast him with the orange juice and try repairing my bruised throat.

"Like going back to black-and-white TV."

"Black-and-white? You're not that old."

"We used to have one in the living room. It was left from the people before us. A big old set, like furniture, with rabbit ears. Mother told me it was fine, that it was just like regular TV. And I believed her. The kids at school, though, they made fun of me. I don't know how they found out. I kept insisting I could see the same colors as them. The whole rainbow. I thought colors were grays, really, just a matter of degree. They told me I was crazy."

"You were."

"Finally one of them had me come over. He didn't like me, no one did, but he had me come to his house just to shove it in my face. He turned on the TV and I remember he said, 'There. Look at that. That's *green.*' Like I was an idiot." ·

"So what'd you tell your mama?"

I wrap a blanket around me. I am shivering.

"She had enough on her mind."

He shakes his head.

"The point is: it was better before. Black-and-white. Colors are an illusion."

"Lock up your daughters," Cooney laughs, resuming his meditation pose. "Ethan Harms is back in town."

"No. I don't mean it that way." I am hurt. "Just because I stopped taking my pills doesn't imply . . . I would never . . ."

But he is no longer listening. He can go away without moving a muscle. My throat keeps swallowing. The toilet bowl looks like *Sunset Over the Grand Canyon*. With nothing else to do, no artificial drug-induced stupor to sink into, I haul out Dr. Roberta Bush's drawing supplies. I look for a love note or candy bar secreted in a corner of the box, anything to make it a more personal gift. It is depressingly empty.

I should be grateful but really it is just a burden, this stack of white paper waiting to be marked up, waiting to be dirtied, first step on its path to becoming garbage. And these sticks, black grime, the same we breathe on a daily basis, collected and pressed into a tube like it is special. I choose a sheet at random and smooth it out on the floor.

I would watch all sorts of things, I resume my monologue, internally now. Farm reports. Religious shows. I was perfectly happy. It never bothered me until I went to that boy's house. Then I was confused. Also resentful that Mother had lied to me, acted like what we did was normal. How we lived. Who we were. Before, I had managed to discount most of what I saw, twist or shoehorn it so it fit assumptions I took for gospel, but just having him say, "Green. That's green," dispelled all those tortured mental maneuvers. It was liberating,

I suppose, but I have never cared much for liberty. Even then I sensed it a double-edged sword.

What is there to draw except what is right in front of you? I sketch six solid bars rising from floor to ceiling. They take shape, evenly spaced barriers of soot with nothing in between.

6.

"Forty seconds," I call.

The guard has already tapped his stick. He is lackadaisical, though, and I am last in line so there is no impatience behind. Fate has once again thrown me in with Littlejohn. I am stuck watching the newbie's back, his slender thighs and boyish buttocks, as he refuses to move. He has not really been showering, more giving himself up to the water, standing under the weak spray and clasping his hands behind his head, refusing to deal with the stony soap, bellying forward so his whole body is flexed. A body hairless and without tattoos, I note. Which is unusual around here. Even Eldridge, who seemed, at first glance, to have aged beyond his markings, turned out to have that creepy anatomical-looking butterfly.

"Time," I say again.

The others here have already moved forward, the last in each line. Soon the hot water will be gone. I look to the guard, but he is no help. He has a typically stupefied expression. I move forward and touch Littlejohn's shoulder.

"Forty seconds. You got to move."

Now I see what he is so proud of. I join, in admiration and disgust, at beholding a member twice the size of any I have ever seen. Perhaps it has to do with his body, so slight and juvenile, the contrast it creates. Uncircumcised, the head wags with intelligence, a dowser's divining rod.

"Hot water's going to go off any minute," I finally find the words. "You got to move."

The swellings from Stanley's beating have gone down but there are other marks, body blows only visible because we are naked and because of his pose, so exposed. Someone has been whaling on him. That, in itself, is not unusual. For many, it passes for pleasure here, both inflicting and receiving pain in a world where there is so little else to trade on. Peering at one blow right above the solar plexus, I can see marks, individual pools of blood originally blue but now purple and orange, so at least a week old.

"Who did this to you?"

The guard taps his stick a final time, harder than before. The water obediently shuts off. I lunge for the last pathetic discharge. Coming between Littlejohn and the nozzle, even though the flow has stopped, breaks him out of his trance. He frowns, looking down, just as surprised as I at his enormous dong. The throb has begun to subside.

"Who's been doing this to you?" I ask, noting other marks now.

Someone is very systematically and methodically traveling over the milk-white landscape of abdomen, stomach, chest, leaving a timeline of suffering, bruises in various stages of efflorescence, so complete that where there is no blotch I assume the damage is recent enough not to have yet risen to the surface.

Littlejohn walks away under his own power, without any of the gasps or flinching one associates with cracked ribs.

"Towel," the guard orders, as I am left alone under the unforthcoming spout.

Don't need a towel, being bone dry, I resist the urge to point out, thanks to you not enforcing the rules.

Instead I hustle into the changing area, a stripped-down locker room where we are given ten minutes to dry and get dressed. Most are already done, having finished before us. Littlejohn passes the threadbare material over his wounds. He must be numb. He takes no special care.

Maybe he bruises easily, I consider.

"You don't need to take that kind of abuse. There's ways to fight back. I could teach you."

He frowns.

"Harms," I remind him. "Ethan Harms. Whoever is doing this to you can be taken care of."

I do not know quite what I am telling him, what exactly I have in mind. Taken care of how? But the words come of their own accord, which I have always trusted as a sign of truth.

His shirt is over the marks now. They are gone as if they never were.

Perhaps he is insensible to pain?

"You sure you're OK?" I confirm.

"I'm good." He is lithe, delicate. He puts his pants on like he is dressing up. "Except for you staring at my joint."

"I wasn't staring. I was trying to take a shower. You took too long."

"Got a lot to clean," he smirks.

"Someone's hurting you."

His back is turned. I sense words enter him better that way, as he is departing, when he is no longer putting on a show of bravado.

"You may think it's necessary but it's not. There's a way out of these relationships, even here. I can help."

He shows no sign of slowing down.

"I can minister to your soul."

The words sound foolish as they leave my mouth. That, too, I take as a positive sign. Attempted good deeds *should* make us feel uncomfortable, *should* be hard, otherwise they would be commonplace occurrences, which they are most assuredly not.

I CLOSE my eyes so the sight of the bars grinding into place, bouncing slightly as they meet their mark, will not depress me. There is still the sound though. The clang. You cannot close your ears.

Disturbed by events, I concentrate on the future, that is to say Heaven, which is all I have to look forward to. Heaven? you ask incredulously, thinking it the last place I have any chance of ending up. But I have been doing penance, sincerely and with a great deal of pain, for far longer than the time it took to commit my transgressions. I have suffered and will continue to suffer until the end of my days. In the meantime I try leading a moral life, which is no easier here than on the outside. Surely I have a shot at redemption. God's mercy in relation to our sins is, I was taught, as big as a football field, on which we are mere ants.

"A sinful ant?" I remember asking Father Bryan. "What would an ant's sins be?"

He was not one for logical argument.

We were in the cemetery doing one of his rubbings. Though young (I realize now), he was already overweight and out of shape. He huffed and puffed as he knelt, just from the mild exercise of passing a chunk of black chalk over a sheet of newsprint.

"Heaven," I persisted, for even then I realized it was my only way out. "What's it like?"

"A mystery," he replied automatically.

"Is my father there?"

"Why do you think your father's dead?"

The dates were beginning to take shape. And the name. They were absences, where the chalk did not reach. More interesting to me was the texture of the stone as it poked through the smooth surface of paper.

"An ant can't sin," I frowned, refusing to let small inconsistencies pass unremarked, unwilling to confront larger ones. "It has no free will."

"Sure it does. It can decide to go here or there. To pick up a piece of leaf or not."

"No. It's part of something bigger. A colony. I read—"

I checked myself. People were surprisingly suspicious when they found out I had read anything. The cookbooks were bad enough. Mother thought they were "sissy," though I pointed out many of them were written by men. "Chefs," she corrected, a lesser, apparently subsexual breed she had much experience with. Now I was exploring, with more circumspection, a whole patch of college texts that had to do with biology and animal behavior. They were higher up on the shelf.

"Ants. People." He waddled forward to bear down on a particularly troublesome spot. "I was just trying to explain to you how God—"

"They're parts of a collective brain," I blurted. I do not know why it was so important to me. My job was to hold the paper. My arms were spread as wide as they could go, embracing the filthy stone. "The queen produces eggs. And each egg tells you exactly what kind of ant it's going to be, worker, warrior, nursemaid . . ."

"Nursemaid?"

"They take care of the larvae. Feed them and keep them clean. But the kinds of eggs she produces are based on what she's fed. It all has to do with the food that's brought from outside. She never goes outside herself. She's . . ."

I wanted to say "disgusting." That was what the pictures made her look like. This huge distended belly, always on her back, pumping out glossy white balls like in a science fiction movie.

"There!"

He managed to get in the person's whole name.

Now came the hard part, carrying the billowing piece of newsprint inside without having it touch anything and get smudged. We held it by either end and coordinated our footsteps, escorting it to the rectory by the back door.

"So her body," I went on, "senses what's out there, based on the food she's given. She can tell everything, temperature, rainfall, what time of year it is, all from the food. And that determines what the colony needs to go forward, to make it thrive. Then she makes the right mix of eggs to meet all those needs. So it's decided on a much higher level. One ant, all by himself, he's got no choice. He's preprogrammed. He can't commit a sin."

"I was speaking metaphorically."

I did not know what that meant. I still do not. It is such an obvious evasion.

We laid the rubbing on the Ping-Pong table. He took a spray can and fouled the air with poison, a mist of evil-smelling droplets. I watched them settle over the crude summary of someone's life.

"This fixes it in place," he explained.

I am not an ant, I decided, watching him.

"Do you faint?"

"At the sight of blood? You got to be kidding."

"Many people do."

"I guess you don't read the papers."

"Some react differently to their own."

"I never made that distinction. It's a river that runs through us all."

Mbaéré shrugs. I am in the Sick Unit, though not sick. Another interesting anomaly is that I am not strapped to a gurney. I am sitting on the edge of an examining table as I would in a regular doctor's office. Blood gushes from the vein of my inner arm, filling glass vials.

"You should be flattered. Warden does not take such a personal interest in most inmates."

"—still don't like it."

"It is necessary that I run tests."

"Do they practice voodoo where you come from?"

He removes the needle and gives me a cotton ball to press down on.

"I didn't mean you personally. I meant in your country."

"My country is a very sad place." He shines a light in my eyes, squeezes the glands on either side of my neck. "Very beautiful as well."

"Just what are you looking for?"

"Seizures can have many causes."

"Do you think it's related?"

The room has a peculiar yellow tinge. Despite the smell and the gurneys, their restraints lying limp as if exhausted by breaking so many men's spirits, I feel a kind of comfort. Perhaps it is being in such close proximity to a human being whose dress and comportment speak of choice rather than submission. The collar of his shirt, appearing above the top of his white lab coat, comes into sharp detail, like a mountain range.

"Open, please."

"I mean do you think there's something wrong with me physiologically that would explain both the spells and my previous behavior?"

He is wielding a tongue depressor.

"It's a possibility. But even if there were, we don't yet have the technology to detect such abnormalities."

"Abnormalities?"

"You've done horrible things. You were aware of them being wrong, weren't you?"

"I suppose."

"Yet you continued to do them."

The balsa wood, as it tamps down, is surprisingly pleasurable, perhaps more for the childhood memories

it evokes than its taste, although who is to say where
one leaves off and the other begins?

"Some would argue you no longer commit crimes
only because you do not have the opportunity."

"No! Ah doan doo tha kine of thing aneemoah!" I
protest.

"Shhh." He soothes me as he would an infant.

"You don't believe me?" I demand, when I get my
voice back, wondering if I was so vehement in my denial
because I knew it would only be semi-intelligible.

"I am saying that an organic neurological problem
would explain why, even if you wanted to stop, you
could not."

"All because of some truffle growing at the base of
my skull?"

"Follow my finger."

I do, but at the same time note the vials of blood
lying casually on a tabletop, each with its little wrap-
around label. It is laughable, the very concept that
something inside me makes me tick or prevents me
from ticking properly; that it can be isolated, treated
or, god forbid, removed, a part of me that is at the
same time not-me. It is slipshod thinking so typical of
the age.

"I think I prefer voodoo. Go to a witch doctor, take
part in a ritual, drink a magic potion or eat the heart
of my enemy."

"And who exactly is your enemy?"

I smile.

"You people romanticize." He unknots the rubber
tubing with a snap. "Where I come from what the
inhabitants need is proper sanitation, not tourists

looking for eye of newt or drinking cups made from men's skulls."

"Why did you take me out of the restraints? It's against protocol, isn't it?"

"I don't care to treat people that way. It's undignified."

"I appreciate it."

"It's undignified to *me*. I'm not a torturer."

He is close to my face. His fingers, his breath, his body heat, register on the thin skin covering my cheek and ear.

"People think you are."

"People here do not 'think' at all."

"It's a pretty persistent rumor. Is it on your résumé or something?"

"It is a perversion of the facts."

"Facts? So something did happen?"

He frowns, unwilling to say more.

"They're questioning me." I do not know why I choose to confide in him. "Trying to get me to talk, to rat out my friend."

"It is my experience that a person can only be made to divulge what he truly desires to say."

"They want to know about a body."

His manner changes abruptly.

"I don't wish to hear such things."

"Park your car in front of any high school."

That is what Mother advised, a suggestion complicated by my being fifteen and not yet in possession of a driver's license, much less a vehicle. But I took everything she said, when delivered in a certain mood, as a mysterious utterance, the type you would receive from an oracle. I brooded over the words at night, in my increasingly cluttered book-lined alcove. Park my car? To accomplish that I would need money to purchase even a secondhand wreck, and I would need not to be *in* high school anymore, for then how could I be outside at the same time? I saw myself, one hand wrapped around the grip of the steering wheel, the other loosely cupped over the stick shift, my foot playing with the gas, the engine vibrating my groin.

The mood she had to be in was one of postcoital trance brought on by alcohol and abandonment. I learned when to knock, always with an offering, ice water, hot tea, depending on the season, careful to keep the noise level low and the light nonexistent. With infinite care I turned the knob and worked the door against dry hinges.

She would not acknowledge me, except to reach out and receive whatever homage I brought. This was now one of the few intersections of our respective days. Mornings, she slept late. I got myself off to school. By afternoon she was gone, "bar-maiding" or "cocktail waitressing," depending on how she felt about her current place of employ. By the time she returned my sole household chore was to make myself scarce, which I did by simulating a corpse stashed behind the free-standing bookcase. But weekend mornings, after one of her rough nights, I would tend to her and she would accept my ministrations, though never letting me see her puffy and, to her critical eyes, ravaged face. She lay propped in the darkened bedroom smoking cigarettes, sipping whatever I closed her pliant fingers around, willing to answer any question.

The idea of my waiting outside the high school came in response to a wondering aloud about girls. They seemed so distant, a herd of creatures that would move off if you got too close. It was impossible to cut one off from the many, and even if you could how would you know which to choose when they seemed all-of-a-piece?

Her answer was hardly meant to be encouraging. It was contemptuous both of the stalker and the prey. The ease, she implied, with which one could have any of these little tarts (her mildest word for a female younger than herself) was matched only by the low esteem in which she held the fool willing to waste his time and money in such a fashion.

I was fascinated by this picture of the world. It was thrilling, despite her grim tone.

"Is that how you met Dad?"

She took a long, moist drag. She had a pumpkin-shaped ashtray she kept in bed, placing it on the covers, between her legs. When she tapped a cigarette or ground out a butt it presented a distinctly unlady-like image. "Jesus Christ," I once heard a man say, listening through the door, and knew exactly what he was reacting to.

"He didn't need to do anything like that."

"Why not?"

"Your father understood women."

. . . which explained both why she gave him her heart and why he stomped on it, or so I interpreted that cryptic remark, one of the few she ever made about him.

It was not so much that she despised the fellow members of her sex as that she saw them bleakly, without gauze or trimmings. She was harder on no one more than herself, criticizing every one of her past actions, right up to the still-visible depression in the far side of the mattress. Men, by contrast, hardly entered her moral universe. They were neither good nor bad, merely obstacles, seductive obstacles, inevitable obstacles, insurmountable obstacles, though to *what* I do not think she could have said. She was being helplessly held back from a goal, a promised land she could not even imagine just dreadfully felt the lack of. She stubbed out the sparks of another still-glowing mistake, gripping the sides of the ceramic pumpkin with her thighs.

"So then what?" I asked, already in the car, school out, the trickle of recent classmates seeping slowly at first, then, the dam breaking, becoming a tidal wave of flesh and spirit. "What do I do next?"

"Well, if you're not stupid," she sighed, implying the jury was still out, "you'll look for a girl with plaid tights, her hair in braids, made up to look like a raccoon, who walks kind of funny, because she has a condition."

"You mean she limps?"

"No. Like the earth is too hot. Like it's burning."

I could see this girl so clearly: awkward, making her way with difficulty, negotiating bumps and valleys others ignored. But she did not see me. She looked straight ahead.

"Do I call to her?" I persisted. "Honk my horn?"

She set the glass I had given her on the sheet, where it tilted precariously, still brimming with ice.

I waited for more, but there was none.

"How was your night?" I asked in a different tone, meaning how much money had she made.

"Good," she admitted.

Her continuing powers of attraction surprised no one more than herself, often unpleasantly. She once confided that she could not say no, that it seemed an act of rudeness, though she had no trouble being rude in other aspects of her life, perhaps to make up for this central absence of self-respect. But tips were what we lived on, so she could hardly complain.

"I know I can't get work. I don't have papers yet. But I was thinking of asking Father Bryan if he had anything for me to do."

She nodded slowly, looking past as if a movie was being projected on the far wall, a cracked, grimy section of plaster interrupted by framed photos belonging to the previous tenants.

"Then you wouldn't have to make as much. Maybe you could cut back on your nights."

She was no longer listening. Her eyes were fixed on the far wall, or what lay beyond it.

This was my plan, nurtured during long silent hours spent plotting escape from the alcove. I would make money, gain a foothold in the world beyond, not just past the bookcase but break out of this ramshackle hothouse Mother had constructed for both of us, with its black-and-white TV and furnishings that bore no relation to past or present.

But my first step toward independence began in frustration. Father Bryan did not take my words seriously. I realized that he had always regarded me as something less than human, more an extension of himself rather than a separate entity. Getting free, gaining even that first sniff of raw arctic air, was not going to be easy.

"What did you have in mind?" he finally asked.

"I don't know."

"What can you do?"

This was unanticipated. I had not considered when fantasizing about a job what my skills were. I was unwilling to examine or evaluate myself. Nothing, it had long been made clear, was the ultimate state to which I should aspire, that of never-having-been. Oddly, this gave me a rather objective perch from which to judge my strengths, such as they were.

"I don't get scared. I show up on time. I don't mind getting dirty."

The last quality had stood me in good stead when serving as an altar boy. There was something repulsively disquieting about everyone's sins being shed, the entire congregation purging itself of accumulated filth before receiving communion. As a participant in the process, lowest on the totem pole, I felt a particular need to clean it all up, to assume everyone's transgressions so that the church itself would remain pure. I remember feeling after Mass in the very opposite of a state of grace, bulging with everyone's bad thoughts and worse deeds, a one-way intake valve for error.

"Well, there are the moles," he said.

For a moment, I did not know what he meant. Yes, there were moles. They made a mockery of the smooth lawn he was attempting to keep between the stones of the cemetery out back. Landscaping a cemetery is a tricky and expensive affair. I had already heard Father Bryan bellyache about it. Very few people paid for "perpetual care" of their ancestors. Gardening companies tended to shun old-style graveyards because the narrow and irregular distances between stones meant their machines could not be used. It was manual labor, clipping and mowing individual hard-to-reach areas. Lately, moles had added an unsightly touch, digging their little tunnels so it looked like the dead were visiting each other, paying calls. Their shrunken, rodent-sized souls, not worthy of ascending to heaven or being sucked down to hell, remained trapped in this rocky, root-choked limbo of bad soil, doomed to create blind passageways for all eternity. That was my interpretation of the evidence. Father Bryan called it an eyesore.

Warming to the idea, he showed me a bunch of traps he had bought but not had the courage to set. Each was a triad of sharpened spikes, spring-loaded, connected to an "activator plate" that sensed motion.

"Here are the instructions." He thrust into my unsure hands a single piece of paper that explained in six languages how to kill. "I'll pay you ten dollars a mole. That includes disposing of them."

He gave an involuntary shudder.

And so I became, at fifteen, unofficially and no doubt illegally, caretaker of the Holy Spirit Cemetery. Much was made of this at a later date, but it bears no relation to what followed. My sole motive was to earn money, to get away. I had no desire to become more of who I already was. All my most strenuous efforts have been devoted to fighting the forces that conspired to send me down the wrong path. If I failed, it was not from lack of trying.

7.

The wait for relief grows. It is over an hour now. Guards are not happy. There are fewer of them because of the flu. Half their time, Harris complains, is spent shackling and unshackling prisoners, "holding their hands" while they shit. I wonder why he is so chatty until I realize it is an explanation for not extending the common courtesy of undoing my restraints.

I edge my way into the Porta Potty, reminded of an astronaut in bulky gear trying to cavort on the moon. It is, despite the gagging odor and cold, a luxury to be alone within a private space, to close a door behind you instead of having it rolled shut. I sit and wonder if I could leave my body behind, waft up through the little vent at the top. Is that what happens at death? Does the soul take a shit, leave its corporeal waste behind?

My cosmic spaceship shudders as Harris whams the outside with his truncheon.

"Bowels do not respond to violence," I mutter.

"What did you say?"

"Nothing, sir."

Someone has carved letters on the ledge where the roll of paper should be. They did not use their fingernail or a scavenged utensil but a finely sharpened blade as is evident from the depth and narrowness of the line as well as how the writing flows. Easy to read, it must have been made by a tool with a handle; not a knife, more likely some instrument used in etching or engraving. The result approaches calligraphy.

THE WALLS WILL COME DOWN it promises in clear, yet almost feminine script.

It could not have been meant for me. I try tem-
pering an irrational surge of enthusiasm. There are at
least twenty separate units. One is directed by a guard,
who decides based on distance and availability. Plus,
the Porta Potties have not been here all that long. The
lettering, cryptic, ornate, a little threatening because of
the force behind that relentlessly gouging point, was
probably made somewhere else, at a rock concert or
construction site.

THE WALLS WILL COME DOWN.

There is also the question of believability. Do I
believe what I see? It is, after all, the same color as the
plastic itself, an indentation, perhaps imagined. Instead
of rubbing my eyes I rub the mold-injected shell and
see the beige swell, swallow the canyon of script until
it is impossible to make out. I blink a few times, trying
to recapture the moment, but it is gone.

"The Walls Will Come Down." A promise or threat?
If it is accurate, how will I fare? Gruesome as this place
is, it provides order, which I thrive in. My crimes were
an expression of order, or so my confused brain thought
at the time. I do not relish the alternative. Lawlessness
is not my element, as it is for some here.

Enslaved at the hands and feet, I look around and
find the roll of paper has hidden itself in the rear corner
of the cubicle. I would do the same, I think wryly, if I
knew what fate lay in store for me. Attempting to turn
in the confined space is impossible. I drop to my knees
and inch toward it with my chin.

"What are you doing in there, Harms?"

"Nothing, sir."

The surface, all filth and grit, transfers itself to my face. I do not care. I am on a mission. Sometimes personal hygiene is all you have left. I am determined to wipe my ass. I nose at the paper enough to push it up against the wall, where it bounces and rolls back. I do this again, and again, until it accumulates enough speed to roll past my supine, panting form and come to rest in a place where, if I can just get back to my feet, I will be able to hook it with my thumb and then somehow transfer it to—

Lying on my back, attempting to wriggle forward and wobble onto my heels, I catch an unused, unlooked-at segment of ceiling, invisible from where one sits. I am transfixed—mouth eyes heart wide open—as instead of an obscure curve of roof I see the universe. A magic book, by sheer chance, has been removed. The dazzling celestial light that shines on the other side, more often hinted at than revealed, reaches me unimpeded. I am bathed in its glow. Transfixed.

"Harms!"

"Almost done," I call.

Snow is an event. We are not dressed for it, of course. There is no call for us to be issued goose down parkas or stocking caps with little pom-poms on top. When it appears, as in a picture postcard, when it has just begun, and we are in the yard to witness, when it chooses to fall *on us*, snow produces a giddy euphoric air. Men stick out their tongues to collect a tiny sip of pristine water. Others squat and examine flakes, amazed by the concept of no two being exactly alike. Crow and I huddle on the bench, but even he, I would like to think, acknowledges the rare occasion, as what I believe the weather forecasters would call a light dusting sugarcoats our ugliness.

Like a foreign city, I convey silently, nodding toward the Porta Potties.

They occupy one-third of the area. Their little roofs have a chalet-like softness from what has already accumulated. They are still hideous, but the way the plastic accepts the coating gives even these mass-produced cubicles an architectural honesty.

I had an interesting experience the other day, I go on. I was taking a crap, looked up, and found a passageway to the world beyond. I saw how, past outer space, outside the darkness that surrounds this Earth, the universe is blindingly bright.

There is not enough to make a snowball, but many people collect it in their hands anyway, just to watch it melt or to delight in the trails their fingers leave.

Can't remember which, though, I mentally sigh. Which unit, I mean.

I scrutinize them. Some have a superficial difference, a spill of paint, a door that does not hang properly, but there are no numbers or names (Bide-a-Wee, Poop's Pleasure) that would enable me to pick the one out of the many.

Crow's eyes stay resolutely fixed on the middle distance, neither yard nor horizon. Four or five strands of gray run through his otherwise black hair. Every once in a while he swallows.

There is a commotion in the far corner, under one of the towers. It is not so grand as a fight, more a scuffle. The sounds of heavy shoes coping with the unexpected slipperiness of new snow mixes with soft, ineffectual punches and grunts. I try ignoring it and focus instead on what Crow sees. I measure out my perception, so it does not stop too soon or extend too far. Is there something out there? Or are his eyes on automatic pilot while his mind supplies visions of another sort?

Just what did Carr do? I ask.

It is a risky question to pose, even psychically. Referring to such an incident may inspire him to reenact it. As a precautionary measure, I place my hand on the back of my neck, pretending to rub out a stiffness.

I mean, did he proposition you? Or was it more like a taunt?

The altercation, even with shouts of encouragement, guards blowing whistles, the thump of reinforcements as more emerge from the main building, is muted and benign. Our exchanges take place in the stillness of a snow globe.

I ask because a friend of mine is being abused. He has marks. It is almost like they are voluntary, though. They are so evenly spaced. But someone is doing harm to him. Whether he is submitting out of fear or a need to be punished I do not know. I want to take him off this path and put him on another. I feel it is essential to my spiritual development.

The benches, as I mentioned, are slabs of wood. Massive trees were sacrificed to our comfort, for which I am grateful. There is something life-giving about even the most desiccated lumber. It is as close to being in a forest as we can ever hope to get. Many have cracked, though, and now the cracks are filling with snow. My eyes try discerning the air itself in the spot Crow is concentrating on, how the molecules churn, galaxy-like crystals of ice zooming past, weak sun managing to shine through. I visualize photons, "packets of energy," a book once told me. It is amazing what sticks to the surface of your brain, no two facts exactly alike.

How did it feel when you turned Carr's head around? What was it like to pluck evil out by the roots? But in the act of doing, did you not take it upon yourself? Don't you sense there is a fixed amount of evil in the world, that all you can do is shift it from one stockpile to another?

I wait but there is no response. I cannot see what he is seeing. My soul recoils at the sheer emptiness. It must be the pills that enable him to stare this way, the experimental ones they use to keep him in a permanent catatonic state.

Snow is falling more thickly now. Soon they will call us in. I brush away a quarter-inch's worth from the bench and notice a crack that has widened in the past few days. The shift in humidity, perhaps. Or a last tree spirit giving up the ghost, forty years on. Idly I run my finger into the newly opened crevice, reaming out the snow, until I come upon something hard. My heartbeat quickens.

You don't have to answer, I convey, more out of politeness now. I was just curious.

I manage to squeeze two fingertips in. It is the end of an object, one that goes deeper. Probably nothing, but even nothing here can acquire an outsized significance. A bottle cap. A bent nail. I have seen men kill for less. We are all magpies, grabbing for whatever scraps of private property we can. Such items are as packed with imagined power as fragments of a meteorite.

The trick, when I pull whatever it is out, is not to have Crow see. True, he does not talk, does not look,

even, but there is no way I am risking this find by
sharing it with another. My fingers tighten around
metal. I get up. It is a gamble. I have to hope it is not
sunk in too deeply, that it comes free with a simple
pull. I cannot stop to examine. Instead I feel the mysterious object, long, thin, and somewhat flexible, resist
briefly then *give* as my fingers adjust and solidify their
grip, all while I hunch over in the cold to shield myself
from the snow. I press the unseen prize tight against
my chest.

I am not sure Crow is aware of any of this. I do
not look back to find out. I walk toward a dead zone
vacated by those who have drifted near the excitement, where guards are now using plastic handcuffs to
truss up several miscreants before marching them off.
There is a parody of "arrest" when one breaks a rule
or merely irritates a person in authority, but no corresponding rights or system for determining justice. A
wrist-bound inmate stumbles, unable to break his fall,
and crashes onto the snowy blacktop. He is kicked for
his troubles, very expertly. When he at last gets up his
mouth leaves a crimson kiss on the white.

It is a tool, as primitive as those left by the Nean-
derthals. A slat of steel, lightweight but tough. One end
has been carefully folded over to provide a handle. The
other is squared off. I run my finger over the edges.
A blade, then, though not sharpened or pointed, not a
knife. There is something more . . . mechanical about it.

We are called over for count. I do not have time to
think. Whoever fashioned this was smart, hiding it in
a bench. That way it could be retrieved when needed.
I was a fool for taking it out and am now stuck with
it as I cannot very well go back and reinsert. I briefly

consider dropping it, but already there are too many people around as we shuffle toward the gate where the shape-up occurs. At the last moment, I feed it up my sleeve, nestling the freezing metal against the tender interior of my arm.

This time I manage to claim my normal place in the wavering line. To my right is Jabbar, a black man whose real name is Preston O'Day; on my left, Robidoux, a native of Louisiana. The Gator, he was dubbed by the press, during his brief spell of notoriety, for certain marks he left. There is a prohibition against facial hair, yet he somehow still manages to project the idea of a bushy red mustache with twisted ends, also a kind of merriment in his eyes. He was, I am sure, charismatic in his day. Now he is a dullard, chewing constantly with nothing in his mouth. The antipsychotics encourage the growth of an invisible sop jaws work mightily against but can never swallow.

"Due to the infraction," the guard announces, "there will be a twenty-four-hour lockdown and suspension of all privileges."

He waits in vain for that to sink in. It is hard to punish us. Yes, you can cause pain, anguish even, but it does not rise to the level of correction. There is no longer a link between one's deeds and any resulting misfortune. The notion is too pervasive. We are inside punishment, living it each day. So extreme has society's disapproval of our actions been that it can only be expressed once. Besides, the way the weather is coming down, we would have been confined to quarters anyway.

"There will also be a cell search," he adds significantly, "commencing immediately."

This produces a faint rumble of resentment. It is purely vindictive, intended not to find weapons or contraband but keep us standing here out in the cold as the once fluffy, greeting-card snow becomes sleet.

I, however, am glad. A cell search now means not another for at least a few weeks, giving me time to figure out what to do with this . . . part, it now feels like, warming up as it becomes comfortable with my skin. Tool? Part? Clue? I know I am making too much of it but one's sadly tattered curiosity creates what it can from the little it is given. I will take it out at night, close my palm around its handle, and try to extract from the crafted shape some sense of purpose.

"Fucking motherfuckers," Jabbar mutters.

I am unclear as to the nature of his crimes. Many of the black folk here (not nearly as high a percentage of the population as in prisons for more mundane offenses) cling to the belief they were convicted unfairly, which may be true for all I know. It makes them more reticent about their accomplishments.

"What you got?" I ask, staring straight ahead.

"Nothing. I don't got nothing. But they *put* stuff there. Just to mess you up."

He stamps his feet and pushes his hands deeper into the waistband of his pants. Snow collects on his wiry hair.

"Put what?"

"Stuff," he insists stubbornly.

Robidoux contributes to the conversation but with the imaginary chunk of meat in his mouth plus his Cajun accent he is largely incomprehensible.

"I used to hide magazines under my mattress," I recall, just for the pleasure of hearing a decently constructed sentence.

"Magazines?"

"Not here. In my room. Growing up. The kind that have a centerfold. Remember them?"

Jabbar looks at me like I am crazy.

"What would *you* do with a woman?" he snaps contemptuously.

"Treat her with love and respect."

He goes back to tromping up and down.

Robidoux spits. I cannot help but look to see if anything comes out, his mouth does such a good job of counterfeiting an obstruction. There is nothing. The lack of intellectual companionship here is worse than the exposure. I withdraw, leaving my body to deal with the elements. I try formulating a plan of survival for getting past the next forty-five minutes. That is the key, to focus on the immediate. Not to think about years or, god forbid, a lifetime, but on visible viable goals you can achieve. Making it to my cell, finding a home for the strange piece of metal.

"If they really want to search for something," Jabbar complains, "they could find what's causing people around here to get cancer."

"Who's got cancer?"

"Everyone! Whole place. Guards. Prisoners." He looks around. We both do, as if by being named the tumors will now be made visible. "They just don't tell you, see? They want you to go quietly."

"Why would they do that?"

Once again he gives me a disbelieving look.

"So you don't cry out. So you don't demand treatment. So you don't make a stink."

"You think you got it, then? Cancer?"

"Oh, I got it," he says, with a strange satisfaction. "I got it good."

We squint. Nothing is visible. The snow has become a diagonal curtain.

Pill dodging becomes a daily ritual. I am not even sure what positive advantage it confers but I have discovered all sorts of tricks to play with my throat, my sinuses, even my eye sockets. Recently I have been able to utilize the last of these by making a tic-like twitch that sends whatever meets the launching pad of my tongue on a wild journey that ends at the entrance to the tear duct.

"Ethan, what's wrong?"

"Nothing." I blink back the burning stream such contortions produce. It was my bad luck to be called in for a session with Dr. Bush right after tray time. "A cold, maybe."

I sneeze loudly. The aftertaste of purged, dissolving pills drains down onto my palate.

She goes back to studying the drawings.

"They're very abstract."

"What do you mean?"

"They're not of anything, are they?"

"Of course they are. They're of the ceiling, the floor, the bars . . ."

"I thought they'd be more personal."

"There's nothing more personal than my situation."

She holds one up. It is of my bed, though I must admit a nonresident would be hard-pressed to recognize that. To the uninformed it is nothing more than a rectangle set at a dangerous tilt.

"What do you think about when you see this?" she asks, as if it is a Rorschach blot. "Ethan? Are you all right?"

I am staring not at the charcoal and paper but her hand, on which sits a circle of gold with a tiny fleck of light. A diamond.

"What the hell?"

"Am I holding it the right way?"

Despite the interrogation table, I make an abortive move to examine the new addition more closely.

"Oh." She puts down the drawing and covers the offending finger with her other hand. "I guess I should have mentioned that."

"Are you engaged?"

"I'm . . ." It puzzles her, the concept. "Yes. I guess I am."

I know I am supposed to say, "Congratulations," but it is not at all what I am thinking.

"It's something that's been going on for a long time. Last week we decided to make it official."

"He asked you to marry him."

"We decided together, yes."

"He didn't ask?"

"He—"

She picks up the drawing again, staring at it differently this time. She is aware, though, that I continue to gawk.

"Is it real gold?"

"I have no idea. This shape here . . ."

"It's my bed."

She tries to set it down. It misses the tabletop and wafts all the way to the floor.

"You can tell, you know, if it's real or not. You can take it to a jeweler."

"That's silly. Why would I want to do that? What difference would it make? We don't have a lot of money."

"Is he a doctor too?"

"Doctoral candidate. No."

She takes it off. That surprises me. How often do you see a woman remove her engagement ring? The flesh underneath is different.

"Is that why you stopped painting your nails? Because you weren't looking anymore?"

"Looking?"

". . . for a man."

"All right," she smiles. "We're going to have to stop this whole line of questioning."

"Why?"

"Because you're not the one doing the research. I am."

"Then ask me something."

She still has not put it back on though. It is in her fist.

"Go ahead," I say. "Do your research."

"The women you killed, why did you do it?"

We have, for so long, avoided this, edged around it. I admire her resolve. Clearly she feels threatened, entering into a loveless unsatisfying union with a eunuch whose idea of an engagement ring is something you slide along a curtain rod. So she attacks, not letting me ride roughshod over her. I like that. It advances our understanding. We are not back to where we were, but deeper. I feel the pathetic prick of that bargain basement stone against her tightened fist.

"If I knew the answer, I wouldn't be here."

"What's that supposed to mean?"

"In this room. Talking to you. You wouldn't be drawn to me and I wouldn't be a figure to invite such speculation, if I knew why I did what I did."

"I'm not drawn to you."

"You're finished with everyone else's interviews, aren't you?"

"I can't discuss other test subjects."

"Don't you ever wonder why you chose this particular area as your field of study?"

"No. I mean, it doesn't keep me up at night."

"Maybe it should."

She closes the notebook. But the ring, the ring has not gone back on her finger. Her hands are open now. It has disappeared, like in a magic trick.

"Why did you kill those women?" she repeats.

"All I can tell you is that at the time it made absolute sense, what I was doing. It seemed like it had already happened, like I was following a pattern that had been laid down specifically for me. *I saw the world.*" These last words do not consciously form. They are spoken through me. "I saw what the world was truly like and what my place in it could be if I acted. If I fulfilled my destiny."

"And what about them?"

"They were fulfilling their destiny too. Look, I am sincerely sorry about what happened. I grieve over it every day. I am remorseful in a way you cannot even imagine. But at the time, you have to understand, it was a dance. That's what it felt like. They entered into it willingly."

"That's disgusting."

"You had to be there."

"You should never say that, in describing what you did. Ever."

"Even if that's what I honestly felt?"

"Especially if that's what you honestly felt."

"Where is it?"

"Where's what?"

"The ring. Where'd you put it?"

Hers is a plastic chair, the kind that stacks. Its seat slopes inward and down. Unlike mine, it is not bolted to the floor. I feel her wetness, her life-giving moisture.

"You're not allowed to ask questions, remember?"

"Next thing you'll tell me is I won't be receiving an invitation to the ceremony."

She looks down to where the drawing lies faceup.

I am suddenly proud, as I certainly was not when I made it. Making it was a chore, like homework. Now, in the context of her puzzlement, it has begun to grow on me.

"This is your bed? But where are you? I don't understand the perspective."

"Upper corner of the cell, against the ceiling, where you view a room from right after you die."

"Why would you draw it from up there?"

"Because it's the last thing I'll ever see."

She bends over to retrieve it.

"What's his name?" I call. "Who's the lucky guy?"

She shakes her head. Her hair takes up the refusal, echoes it. That is when I see, so hard have I been focusing on the ring, trying to track it down, how she has pulled off the tight elastic band that holds back her hair. Both must be in her lap, I theorize, the ring that was on her finger and the ring that bunched her hair, pulled the skin taut over her cheekbones. So we each have a ring, a claim on her, the fiancé and me.

"I don't see how it hurts to ask his name. It's just common courtesy. I thought we had evolved beyond strict question-and-answer."

"Seth."

She is a totally different person with her hair down, younger, almost a kid, angry, leaning forward now, ferreting out secrets, not afraid to reveal her own.

"OK, I told you his name, now you tell me *hers*. And don't . . ."—she nods to a tremor that is beginning to develop in my arms, in my hands—". . . don't pull any of that seizure shit. Don't have one of those conveniently timed 'spells' to get out of confronting what you did."

"That's not why I—"

"Tell me about your first, Ethan."

"I don't give them numbers."

"Her name was Anne."

"How did you know that?"

"I know about all of them. You're a subject."

"Then why ask? If you already know."

"Because I want to hear you say her name!"

She comes in low, tries to see up, tries to see into me. I can smell her. I am somewhat abashed at what she might sense about my own appearance. Restrained in one area, I am asserting myself in another. I shift uncomfortably.

"Seth is a terrible name."

"Anne Greenaway."

"Yes."

"What did you do to her?"

"Nothing she didn't want."

"That's bullshit."

"Like I said, you had to be there."

"I'm here now. Tell me about it. Tell me what you did."

"Nothing you and Seth haven't tried if you're two normal healthy human beings. It just got out of hand is all."

"You can't even say her name."

"I don't say it because I don't want to defile it. I left her in a state of perfection. That's the way I'd like to keep it, to show respect."

She opens the notebook again, I think to write, but then pushes it toward me, hard. It bruises my knuckles.

"If you can't say her name, maybe you can draw her for me."

"I can't draw. You just saw that."

"Cunt."

"I beg your pardon?"

"Last time you drew a cunt for me. That's what you thought it was, right? That's why you got so upset. You tried drawing a butterfly and it ended up a cunt."

"What kind of language is that, for a doctoral candidate?"

"Show me her face."

The spell is still here, in my fingers. Despite what she accuses me of, it is real. They fumble with the pen. I press my forearms against the table, trying to choke off the shakes.

"I can't draw a face."

She waits.

There is writing. Last time she turned it over to a blank page. Now, however, in her haste, she allows me to read one of her notes. Her penmanship is abominable, a backward slant, words battling gale force winds. I have to decipher quickly, surreptitiously, knowing she will snatch it away if she sees.

dysphoria/quasi incestuous

"Quasi," I mutter.

"What?"

"Nothing."

A thing is or is not. "Quasi." A like word for "like." A dog chasing its own tail.

"He takes care of me just fine," she says. "That's what you're wondering about, isn't it? Seth and me together. Our sex life. We're very compatible."

"I am not wondering about anything."

I squint, trying to make out more of what she has written, but where it is not illegible it aspires to the level of gibberish. Something about *maniac psychosis.* Or perhaps *manioc,* that root you pound to make tapioca.

"You don't like it when I talk this way, do you?"

There is a painful situation in my pants. Spells usually take care of it. I wake and it is gone. But because I am fighting the seizure, directing all the trials and tribulations my body is undergoing back down into my fingertips, my groin strains against the void. Men are so exposed. Far more so than women. Luckily women are too blind to see.

"All right, Ethan," she relents. "Calm down."

My fingers have been frenziedly marking up the page. Not a face, just lines, this way and that. Yet they seem to have meaning for her. Her voice softens, soothes. She takes the notebook away, even though I am still twitching. They are slashes. Each one goes deep.

"What's wrong with Seth, as a name?" she asks casually.

"It's in the bible," I gasp. "He's the third child of Adam and Eve."

"Really? I didn't know that. I thought they just had Cain and Abel."

"Exactly. He's superfluous. Nobody knows what happens to him. Nobody cares."

She has moved the notebook around. My fingers are strangely calm, the spell having passed, though I could not vouch for their behavior if they were given free reign. As for my private parts, they are damp, chunky. She does not even know what we have been doing. She is so inexperienced.

"Sorry," she says.

"No, no. My fault."

"You said you were getting sick."

"Just a head cold. I've had a temperature, the last few days."

"Would you like me to give you another mindfulness exercise?"

Dysphoria. I do not even know what the word means but I know it is incorrect. "Dys" implies a malfunction. An inability. I am dys-nothing. I work just fine, in the areas that count, in the areas that most people ignore entirely.

"Concentrate on your skin. See it as the single largest organ in your body. Can you do that?"

She is looking at me. This must be how she is, after. I do not have much experience with after. Most of my encounters have not included that phase.

"Now feel the air touching that organ. Feel it being surrounded by atmosphere. Do you feel that?"

To answer yes or no would be a lie. It is horrible, the way I am being held by her gaze. Probed. I make a slight motion with my buttocks. The bolted leg of the chair squeaks.

"Now feel it breathe. Breathe through your skin, in and out. Feel the permeable nature of what covers you. Feel how there is no finite barrier separating you from the outside world. Do you feel that?"

Quietly she closes the notebook, closes the cover on the frenzy I have drawn. She puts her ring back on her finger and the ring of elastic back in her hair. She leaves, taking a little bit of me with her, through the doors, through the gate, to the parking lot. I am there. No finite barrier. Loose gravel crunches under her shoes. One pebble is kicked, bounces into the distance. I am still there, with her. It is a miracle. The invisible thread between us does not break. It plays out and out and out.

8.

Laundry is another instance of the good old days gone bad. We were in the past allowed to perform the simple task of feeding our sheets and dirty clothes into washer-dryers before it was decided to have everything sent away and returned in antiseptically sealed plastic bags. The room is still here, with its ancient rusting machines, now used only as a drop-off and pick-up spot. No longer is one's linen one's own. Bedding is grabbed from a towering stack. Shirts, pants, socks, and underwear are laid out in piles, sorted by size. This has led to unintended consequences. Think what it is like

to have no identity as expressed by the items covering your body, no easy familiarity with the fabrics in
constant contact with your skin. Punishment, you say?
But if my clothes are not in some visceral sense mine I
must look for other ways to affirm my existence, more
disruptive proofs.

As in the shower, we proceed at timed intervals,
though not so rigorously monitored since there is no hot
water to be apportioned. You leave your cell, clutching
dirty laundry, maintaining a set distance from the man
in front and behind. We are not issued bags, and the
pillowcases are woefully inadequate. The hug required
to keep individual garments from spilling out is sadly
sensual. Never is it made more apparent no one else
will have us.

Approaching the corner, I hear Stanley, his soft,
unmistakable wheeze. He is talking to Shel, Richard
Shelburne, a killer of prostitutes.

"You got a problem?"

"Don't even know what it is," Shelburne whines.

"That's none of your business."

"If it's none of my business, then why do I have
to—?"

"Just do what I say."

None of this is unusual. Stanley has his little cote-
rie of weaklings. Although I have no idea what they
are discussing it sounds like the typical overwrought
social interaction that takes place here, violence and
power always on the lookout for new ways to express
themselves. I drop a sock to delay my entrance. From
the floor their barely audible voices travel more clearly.

"What if he says no?"

"Then you scoop out his eyeballs."

Footsteps approach. I straighten up just in time.

It is Shelburne, with his neatly organized load. He is a strapping man, tall, with muscles and hair in lieu of brains. A coward, he left those women in lonely stretches of highway wilderness, the stunted scrubland and swamp you watch as your car drifts from its lane. He stowed them in shallow poorly dug graves, got caught because one fought back, was maimed but not killed. She crawled right up out of the sod, at which point he panicked and fled. Seeing me, he frowns, then quickens his pace.

I proceed on to the laundry room. Stanley is pretending to choose, although there are no choices. You cannot even finger the possibilities as you would a display of fruit. The plastic coating renders them identical and meaningless.

"Small?"

Stanley's voice, worn smooth by prison, is air blown though a tube, not formed by tongue, teeth, or lips. It gets twisted into sense at the last minute.

"Medium," I say.

He continues to offer me the same shirt, freak product of an industrial-strength off-site dryer, fit only for a dwarf.

"Go ahead." He shakes it slightly, goading. "See if it fits."

"You beating on the newbie?" I ask.

Although I make it a policy to be innocuous, never cause a stir, there is no point in deferring. The only play a bully understands is calling his bluff. He smiles to show off bad teeth, as if a bunch of brown stumps could make me shake. I do not slow for an instant, come right up beside him. That is the cue for him to move on. If the guard was doing his job, not staring himself a new navel, he would tap his stick or issue a command and Stanley would be forced to retreat, pushed out by my presence. Instead we are afforded a moment.

"Newbie?" he wonders, all innocence. "Why would I do that?"

"Just back off."

I grab my allotment with less care than usual, but still exercise some discrimination. The sad truth is we *do* choose, even though there is no choice to be made. We go through the charade of exercising our rapidly atrophying taste. It is one more descent through ever-deepening levels of degradation. This time, though, I am hardly paying attention. I am alert, ready to defend myself, all while assuming an air of rigidly enforced calm.

He giggles, watching.

"What's your problem, Stanley?"

"—gonna eat you for lunch."

"That would be a switch," I point out.

"Not me. Him!"

"Watuski," the guard warns, finally waking up.

"Lunch," he laughs, bending over. It is the punch line to a joke I have unwittingly told. "He's going to eat you for lunch."

"Who?"

"Super Glue."

"Mess with him, mess with me," I hear myself warn.

This only sets off one of his patented streaks of loony-bin hilarity.

The guard taps his stick. It is as effective as a blow, so habituated are we to the consequences of disobeying. Our feet start of their own accord.

In fact, I do not care one way or the other for Littlejohn. Not personally. What I feel, as I tried explaining to Crow, is a calling. I must rescue him. He has fallen into the slot left vacant by Eldridge. I have been assigned this boy who is on the cusp of manhood but fighting it. What were the transgressions that sent him here but an unwillingness to accept maturity, turning what should have been an encounter between two adults into a perverted form of horseplay, of youthful hijinks gone horribly wrong?

Sealing their mouths shut with Super Glue, I chide, in my mind. Were you thinking of Super Balls and Silly String and all those other toys six-year-olds play with?

My role is that of messenger, not participant. I have to make him see he has sinned. Not in a thunderous, guilt-inducing way. I am the last person to climb the steps of the pulpit and judge my fellow man, but by slowly unknotting the twisted, strangling mess his morals have gotten themselves into. No doubt the boy is, for starters, sexually confused. But sex is only a manifestation. The underlying cause is a distance from God. He thinks he has something special down there, growing riotously, but really it is just death, making inroads, algae taking over a pond where there is no oxygen, no Father.

Walking back, I hug my laundry with a firm, defensive grasp as if I am in danger of falling, as if its soft, maddeningly coated nature is the only thing keeping me from spiraling into the pits of hell.

Back "home" (the word mockingly pops up in the course of everyday thought), I tear off the molecule-thin layers of plastic and create a large rectangular mask which I press over my entire face. This is one of the few forms of suicide available, the other being to stretch a sock and hang oneself from the top of the cell, which is harder than it sounds. I breathe in against the barrier and feel the wrapping get sucked into my throat. When one can control so few of the external factors in one's life it is a pleasure to have a say over oxygen. I breathe out, the concave covering flipping to convex. Is this akin to what his victims felt? I imagine their lips glued shut while his fingers, more out of curiosity than sadism, pinched off the only other available airway. Victims, of course, is a loaded word, one invented by the press and prosecution. I can assure you that the perpetrator of a crime does not feel he has chanced upon a victim. The tie is too intimate. You are in this together. Finally *in*, what, for the other 99 percent of the time, we all so carefully avoid, avert our eyes from, what we spend our lives tiptoeing around. It is the ultimate moment of connection, of which the sex part is only one small aspect.

The plastic is well down into my mouth now. It is a wad, adapting itself to the interior, filling every crevice. If I draw it in a little deeper, the swallowing mechanism will take over, dragging it down where I can no longer grasp an edge and fish it out. This is what they felt, his fingers pressing on either nostril, his angelic golden-haired visage shutting out what little light was left to penetrate their eyes, which were being smothered as well, seeing mostly red, the pounding of blood, and, lower down, the stiff penis, finding no relief anywhere, only more tension and frustration, that sad stick that is the most commonly remarked-upon feature of death by asphyxiation.

I spit it out, expectorate it like a huge gob of phlegm. It shoots up in the air and lands wetly on my chest, what should be disgusting, but in my panting, help-lessly grateful reentry to the world is beautiful.

"See this one here," Cooney sighs, "he looks like me, or he's been made up to look like me, but I get no sense he's real. He could be a dummy in a window display for all I can tell."

He often resumes conversations (that is to say maunderings about himself) after week-long gaps, as if I have been brooding over the same issues as he, as if his life is more important to me than my own.

"Now here's who I picked." He holds up a photo, not an eight-by-ten-inch actor's portrait, an actual pic-ture ripped from a magazine. "But when I mentioned him to the producers they didn't even respond."

I stare at my hand, confirm I am still alive.

"Why wouldn't you pay to see this man in a movie?"

"Because he's a gorilla." I squint across. "Or a baboon. What's the difference anyway?"

"The guy standing next to the ape, you moron."

I prop on one elbow to get a better look. There is indeed a man, barely visible. He is more successfully camouflaged than the gorilla or baboon next to him. I can barely make out his features, so hidden are they in facial hair and shadow. He poses jauntily beside the primate, which is his same height. His hand rests on its shoulder.

"She's female," Cooney says proudly. "She could snap off each of those fingers like a dry twig."

"Why doesn't she?"

"Because she loves him, obviously." He gazes at the picture, lost in admiration. "He has introduced her animal soul to love."

"Is he an actor?"

"Hell, no. That's the point. He's an anthropologist. Like myself."

I lie back. The air in my throat is disgusting. It has all kinds of sickly additives that the short break from breathing has made me aware are not natural, not in the inevitable order of things, but unique to this place. It is not enough to go off pills, I realize. One has to go off respiration as well.

"Sexy bastard, isn't he?"

"You saying he had sex with her?"

"With the monkey? That is obscene," he exclaims admiringly. "You have a sick mind, Ethan."

I could have succeeded, could be dead now, and Cooney would be having the same "conversation," addressing himself to my corpse.

"You were dreaming, before."

I face the ceiling, avoiding his eyes, lying still so my body will not reveal its discomfort.

"When?"

"Some night. A while back. Like you were being attacked."

"—wouldn't know," he says curtly.

"You said a name. Wendy? Candy? I think it was Wendy."

He is silent. I take the wet ball of plastic wrapping, still clear in that mysterious way that does not allow you to see through, and brush it aside, send it rolling onto the floor.

"You were tearing at your chest like she'd got you in some kind of grip."

"You should've woke me."

"I thought maybe you were having fun."

He laughs.

"It was surprising," I go on, "to hear you call out a name. I thought they were all laid to rest."

"I got nothing on my mind except this male model actor-type they want."

"So they're all present and accounted for? The brides?"

"Yup," he answers uncertainly.

It is rare we touch upon this area, so sensitive to us both.

"Candy?" I wonder again.

"Wendy." It comes out unwillingly, a long-trapped bubble rising to the surface.

"Old girlfriend?"

"You might say."

And that is all. All it takes. His mind returns to problems of casting and I reacquaint my diaphragm with its duties, hauling in lungful after lungful of poisoned air. Someone begins to scream or more likely has been screaming the whole while. I try following it through the din. The screamer pauses to breathe, then begins again; a thin, solid, heartfelt screech, like fingernails on a blackboard in the outside world but, here, hard to disentangle from all else that is going on.

A storm closes off the yard, makes a bad situation worse. With the toilets still frozen, several Porta Potties are dragged inside where they clutter the already narrow halls. The resulting cabin fever is hard to describe. It is a hollowing out. You do not realize, until deprived, how essential sky, sun, and wind are to maintaining your rational sense of being.

To Ethan Harms,

The only letter I receive in response to the volley I sent out earlier is from Mrs. Mulgrew, our neighbor all through my childhood, or so the return address indicates. But when I open it, I discover it is from a man purporting to be her nephew. His Aunt Susan, is *"no longer able to write.*

"But she did want to answer your questions. Your mother has not lived upstairs for almost a year. My aunt knows this because she used to collect her mail when it was left in the entranceway and hold it for her. She says your mother or her friend would come by and get it every month. She recognized your letters in particular, she says, because of the postmark and stationery. About three months ago, though, the mail for your mother stopped coming. My aunt assumed that she had finally gotten around to notifying the post office of her new address."

"But that doesn't explain my letters getting returned," I object.

"As for your asking if Mrs. Harms is in the hospital, my aunt has not been a nurse for many years, so there is no way of her knowing that. I should warn you that none of this information is guaranteed 100% accurate as my aunt's memory has begun to fail. She still lives alone but receives visits from a home health care professional. In addition, I come around most evenings. When she showed me your letter and I asked about Jen Harms (I had no idea that you were the people upstairs, at the time I was probably too young to be told) she seemed to confuse her with the family who lived there before you, when my aunt was much younger. They

*must have made quite an impression because I had trouble
even getting her to focus on what had become of your mother,
when she left, and with who* [sic.] *This surprised me since,
of course, you are still spoken of a great deal in town. I guess
my aunt wanted to layer over the memory with something
more positive.*

"Hope this helps!"

I read the letter over several times, then sound
it out backward. I also try stringing the first letters
of each word together, hoping they might contain
a secret message smuggled past the prying eyes of
prison authorities. But after all this examination only
two words retain any meaning: "friend," as in "your
mother and her *friend*," and "who," as in "when she
left and with *who*." These tiny sounds set up shop in
my brain and, though they say nothing and do nothing, make it impossible for me to think about or act on
anything else.

Who is this so-called "friend" and what has he done
to my mother? Taken her from home, apparently, the
only one she and I ever knew; snipped the last remaining string that connects us, depriving her of my sage
counsel and me of her unconditional love. Is he holding her prisoner, this Mr. Clean with his Southern
Comfort? What hoops is he making her crawl through
to satisfy his sick desires?

Dear Mr. _____,

I do not know his name. He has used Mrs. Mulgrew's
return address and the signature at the bottom of the
letter is incomprehensible.

*Thank you for your letter and the insights it contains.
The family preceding us on the third floor was indeed intriguing. I felt it too. We were like the survivors of a catastrophe,*

Mother and I, walking through their abruptly abandoned lives, staring at pictures meant for other eyes, following paths worn in the carpet by alien feet, reading books purchased to satisfy an unknown curiosity. Sometimes, when I consider the turn my life has taken, I think it was perhaps their doing, the people who were here before us, that I was obliged to perform certain deeds by a secret contract drawn up without my consent, though what reward could have been offered in return for the endangerment of my immortal soul I cannot imagine.

I stop, realizing this nonentity of a nephew has no interest in such ruminations. In fact his entire letter is really a roundabout way of telling me to get lost. If only I could! There is no way to geographically lose one's self in a correctional facility. I know every inch of hallway, every piece of grit on its floors. I once watched a small lump of bird excrement in the yard for weeks at a time, charting its decay until, when it finally was not there, I felt the loss of a landmark.

Of course, if this was true, I would have been far too young to grasp the consequences of my actions. I would not be responsible. Mother must have spoken for me. That is one of the (many) reasons it is imperative I—

The lights cut out, which is just as well. It is imperative I what? The resolve I have summoned goes slack. Another long night has begun. Lately the prohibition against talking after lights-out has been flouted. I do not know if this signals a general loosening of people's respect for the rules or if it has always been going on and my ears have just become sharp enough to pick out the bits of whispered conversation. A third, more intriguing possibility, is that what I am "hearing" is on a psychic, spiritual, mystical level, tapping into the vast neural network of my fellow sufferers.

People hiss half-phrases, barely distinguishable from steam in the pipes, which are then picked up and repeated, twisted, embellished, contradicted, rolling from one row to the next until the entire block echoes with a barely intelligible roar, that of the ocean perhaps (I have never been) or a nearby interstate. To my recently sensitized ear it is a primordial soup of rumor and fact, lies and truth, a spawning ground, a matrix of data:

"Event," someone insists, "in the yard." "Who the fuck—?"

"Why we can't." "*Nuclear* event." "—kiss my fucking nuts."

"Why they won't let us." "Not the snow." "Nuclear event?"

"Nuclear *power* plant." "Asshole." "Downwind."

"A nuclear power plant?" I echo, shocked. "If that's true, then—"

"It's a *meltdown*." "—why we can't go in the yard." "Kiss my—"

The talk ebbs and flows, cuts off and resumes elsewhere, sloshing in its simultaneity. It is like being inside a brain if a brain operated with words instead of thoughts.

"—wake up dead." "Atomic radiation." "Grow you a second set of balls."

"What about safety?" I demand. "If there is a risk of radiation, we should be notified."

"Food too." "Food's fucked." "Harms fucks his mother."

"That's a fucking lie!" I whisper fiercely.

"Fallout," someone explains. "That's why they won't let us in the yard."

"For how long?"

"It's off-limits, until the radiation dies down."

"What for?"

"For safety."

I am aware of invisible rays, evil isotopes, bouncing at me from all directions. I can feel them. Safety. What a joke. If we were caught in a storm of radioactivity what would they do? Move us? To where? I listen to the murmurs of ignorance and pain. My heart races.

The found object from the yard I have wedged into the seal where the base of the toilet meets the floor. That way if it is discovered I can claim it is part of the assemblage, a piece of scrap a careless worker left behind during the installation. Now, under the cover of absolute darkness, I creep over and ease it out. The squared-off edges are oddly comforting. I lie back down, trying to calm myself, holding it tight like a teddy bear.

Heartbeats thud against the wall. I have only a finite number of these and yet they pass with no meaning, no accomplishment. After a time, I sleep, or perhaps just stop being aware. I could not prove, during these intervening hours, that I existed. My life passes over me, featureless, a starless sky. When I wake, the steel talisman is still clutched in my hand. It is much later now. The sea of talk has been replaced by a troubled silence. With a frustration vaguely related to thwarted desire, I get up and scrape the blade-end against the door, against the face of the lock, which really does have a face, even in the dark, a taunting little hole with screw head eyes. It mocks me. I try to wipe away its grin. The tool, though, is no match for the hardened casing. I cannot even leave a scratch. The edge skitters along the surface, gives up, and slips into a crack along the side, where the bolt rests.

Immediately, before I can withdraw it, there is a click. Not a natural sound. My ears know all the natural sounds this place produces. This click, though superficially similar to a million others, resonates in a unique way, as if it took place in my body rather than the armature of the lock.

Pry bar, the more objectively cool disinterested portion of my mind notes, flexing the supple metal so it burrows behind the bolt. The lock is electric but there is still a manual component. This is its purpose. Like the jimmy you use to open a locked car.

Random sounds punctuate the quiet. A shriek tears the dark in half. A ripping of brain tissue. Someone weeps. The noises I make are minuscule by comparison. The bolt objects just for a moment, then shoots back.

I stay frozen, crouched before the door. My fingers slowly draw out the slat. It is supple and beautifully intact, a fine, precision-tooled device. I close my hand over the metal, shield it with newfound respect.

Now what?

My fingers tighten around the bars, give a sharp pull. All this is still in the realm of the theoretical.

The door slides.

A gale-force hurricane hits me, a hallucination, the concept of space where before there was nothing. Still unwilling to accept what I have done, I pass my hand through the invisible barrier and wait for an alarm to go off. Instead there is just the low-level cricket-chirp

of men masturbating, calling out from nightmares, far-
ting, sneezing, spitting.

I recoil, avoid the trap, yank the door shut. The lock
clicks into place. I test the bars to make sure I am well
and truly safe, stow the tool, and retreat to the corner
of my cell, as far from the door as I can get. I cower,
considering my life, which has taken this new, disturbing turn.

9.

With the yard off-limits and all of us going crazy
from lack of activity even a group as unenlightened
as the guards realizes something must be done. There
is another comparably sized space within the facility,
the assembly hall, where, years ago in more financially
flush times, we watched movies projected onto a white
screen. That in turn was replaced by several dusty tele-
visions retailing more intellectually cramped offerings
before Entertainment Night was discontinued entirely.
But the hall remains, a small stage and rows of bolted-
down seats. This is now offered as a makeshift refuge,
an outlet valve, though the crowded aisles and repulsive wire-crossed ceiling can hardly be compared to
our beloved patch of outdoors. We are encouraged to
distribute ourselves throughout the area. It is amusing
to see how individuals try to reclaim their yard person-
alities, some hopping on the stage to strut and pose,
others lurking in the corners. Crow and I sit next to
each other. He barely registers the change, staring, as
always, out of himself, pouring his soul into whatever
it is he sees, in this case the old gone-gray screen, once

again pulled down, reliving its glory days, expecting at any moment to be bathed in a million colors.

Stanley, true to form, finds the indoor equivalent to his solitary bench, commandeering the lectern from which we were occasionally informed of changes, always for the worse, in the regulations that governed our lives. It is a bit of a shock to see his Halloween-mask features, his slack lips and holes-for-eyes, leering out at us from the podium's place at the edge of the stage, as if Warden himself has been hideously transmogrified.

Feeling expansive, I start mentally chatting to Crow about my early romantic adventures.

I was never good at it, I confide. But that's what kept me interested. People to whom it comes natural, they don't stay engaged. They take it for granted. Me, every step of the way was a struggle. I was tongue-tied. And Mother was no help at all. It's almost like she was setting obstacles in my path, telling me all these unpleasant truths. At least I assumed they were truths. Maybe they were just . . . unpleasantries.

There are, of course, the inevitable troublemakers. Some cannot cope with even the absurdly limited amount of freedom the new setting provides. Hodge, an annihilator of small children, which pretty much makes him an outcast here, takes exception to one of the chairs and tries uprooting it from the floor. They are surprisingly tough, these pressed-wood backs with seats that flip down. The guards intervene but he has already received quite a bit of damage from its stubbornly unyielding form. How can a piece of institutional furniture give a man a bloody nose? I wonder, as they drag him off.

Men will stick it anywhere, I resume. That's what she told me. She was so dismissive of the whole operation. I couldn't square that with what I saw, not just her and her beaux, but with the feelings I harbored, which seemed legitimate to me, the most legitimate feelings I had ever known.

I am happily reminiscing, trying to breathe through my mouth as Crow is smelling even more antisocial than usual, when he stops me. I cannot say how. He simply stares more intently, if that is possible.

What? I frown.

He is fixated on the screen. It is moving. Perhaps he thinks there is a ghost in the room. It is one of those phantom breezes, not just penetrating our inadequate clothing or whipping up a twister of lead-based paint flakes but causing the site of all those hokey Hollywood dramas to writhe convulsively.

Just the wind, I assure him.

That is when the riot starts.

Several guards have escorted Hodge out, leaving a weaker presence. Then there is a silence, one of those empty spots you run across in your day, or that Crow carries with him all the time, a silence extending to the entire population. Everything stops, the milling of aimless men, the clueless cud-like chewing of our keepers, even the packets of light seeping from the drooping, naked bulbs that hang down out of the ceiling, all their workings exposed. My eyes are drawn instinctively to a guard being relieved of his truncheon. It takes an achingly long time to slide loose but, once freed, assumes a life of its own. Other inmates, I check briefly around, are doing the same. Four or five at least. One—I do not feel comfortable naming a particular member of

the community—bears down on his captor, driving
him back, using the club crosswise against the man's
throat. It is not an effective attack. There is too much
space behind. The guard is pushed, avoids having his
windpipe crushed, and stumbles. They go down in a
heap, the prisoner on top flailing away, not even pulling back and using the baton as it is intended, never
connecting with any actual blows. It is more a show
of frustration. I find myself rooting as at a sporting
event. Then my attention is distracted. All around us
mayhem is breaking out. Some are much more effective with the weapons they have seized, swinging with
joyful abandon, not caring whom they hit, not caring
if the blow is delivered with concentrated force or on
the backswing. They are carving out space. I identify
with that. It is every prisoner's dream to increase the
area that is himself, which shrinks to such a pathetic
degree here, less even than the physical limits of his
body. Something crashes from the stage. The lectern is
toppled. It lands precisely upside-down. Little wheels,
visible now in tarnished brass housing, spin. I turn to
Crow. There is perhaps glee in his eyes unless it is a
reflection of my own.

Now the silence gives way to noise. Everyone bel-
lows, expelling the servitude that has worked its way
into the lining of our lungs. Confronted by all this suddenly sincere feeling, I do not know where to look. I am
deeply moved. There are vibrations running through
the floor. They emanate from a prisoner very ener-
getically and methodically stomping a guard's jaw. He
goes about it in workmanlike fashion, circling the prone
scrambling figure, looking for the proper angle, knowing exactly where he wants the impact to land but at

the same time sporting a dreamy "elsewhere" expression, that of a peasant treading grapes. And indeed, by the end, quite a bit of liquid has been produced. The most picturesque moment is when the guard, pleading, holds up his hands in supplication. It is like something out of a religious painting. Yet does he not recognize this as a gesture he has been on the other end of countless times?

"Look!" I call, though my policy with Crow is not to speak out loud. But in the midst of all this shouting I am afraid our silent connection will not suffice.

Stanley has walked to the center of the stage. There is directly beneath him a scrum of bodies. He is elevated, four or five feet above the fracas. He turns his back on us, the audience, and lowers his pants. By now, more guards are appearing. I do not have to turn, I can hear them, their whistles, their boots, their radios. I clutch the little wooden arms on either side of my chair. We are flying, all of us together, a rocket ship zooming through space. Stanley faces the movie screen, which continues to billow.

"That's where God would be if it was an altar," I explain to Crow.

I cannot see Stanley's private parts, for which I am profoundly grateful, but watch with pride the high arc of urine he sends onto the screen. It leaves no color, just darkness, but the sound, even with the distant alarms, the splintering of wood, and now the inevitable clank followed by pops as canisters of gas explode, is marvelously clear.

At last, a real diagnostic test, I note with appreciation.

His bottomless bladder creates a crude ink blot for *them* to interpret.

"What do you see?" I imagine demanding of the many psychiatrists who have put the question to me over the years. I would like to strap their heads in position, clamp their eyelids open, so they could truly take in Stanley's piss marks at the center of all this cruelty and ask them, "What does that remind you of? An elephant? Your mother? A sunset? Really? How interesting."

The gas cloud induces coughing. Rubber bullets begin to bounce off surfaces. They are a health hazard, a good way to lose an eye. I slide down, pull Crow with me. The lights go out. My last vision is of Stanley, still fire-hosing away. Then, after mounting chaos, comes the charge, the thud of bodies.

There is, of course, no apportionment of blame. We are all culpable, even those of us who did nothing. To be, is to be guilty. Whatever summary punishment is meted out we accept uncomplainingly.

Besides, it was well worth it, I judge, perhaps a half hour later.

Bound-in-back wrists make it hard to stay upright. Rubber bullets litter the floor like ball bearings. We get herded along, the last group to be removed, late-arriving reinforcements from the main building too shell-shocked to do more than slam whoever does not keep in line. Everyone is wheezing. The gas is slow to clear. We are not permitted to look around. Looking around is particularly forbidden.

"Eyes front!" Lanza screams.

Sergeant Lanza, I feel like greeting. Back from the flu? How are you feeling? No worse for the wear, I hope.

I am full of good cheer, in a surprisingly forgiving mood.

"Move, you motherfuckers!"

I suppose they are committing the first of their revenge atrocities. That is why we are not permitted to gawk. It is none of my concern. As we approach the door there is a more serious group, senior administrators, effectively shielding from our view the last seat at the end of a row.

"Eyes front!"

I cast a quick glance back to see one officer push heavily on his knees. He rises, leaves a gap in the circle through which appears, for an instant, Mitra. It takes my mind a moment to process, by which time I am gone again, shuffling forward, being roughly handled, trying not to trip and lose my front teeth. Mr. Mitra. What was he doing here? Just his head, I confirm. Not the rest of him. His carefully parted black hair. Those glasses, slightly askew. His puzzled, intelligent expression. Mouth and eyes wide open. And then nothing. Just his head. Visual shorthand. His head *severed*, the word now comes to me. His head a free-standing object placed neatly, squarely, on the worn seat of an old-fashioned fold-down chair. And all the guards standing around. His solitary, sliced-at-the-neck head. And them debating how best to reattach him.

The body is not found until several days later. It is stuffed in a little storage area beneath the stage. We are confined to quarters but conversation swirls. How was he cut in two so efficiently? No weapon, no pool of blood. I am reminded of but do not share the story of the executioner so sure and swift that those sentenced to die did not realize they had been decapitated until they tried to walk away from the chopping block.

I decide to draw, not another picture but a rubbing of my cell floor, its rough surface, the black of the charcoal mixed with white. After all, my floor is as close to a tombstone as I am likely to get. I cannot depend on Mother to arrange for a proper funeral should she have the misfortune to outlive me. The odds are I will end up bone-gravel, a shoebox sitting unclaimed on a high shelf. I scrutinize the paper's rendering of pure pattern looking for dates. Surely the hour of my death is hidden before me, in plain sight.

"You."

Guards are standing outside my cell. They are unlike any I have ever seen. Their uniforms are different, still vaguely military but darker, with unfamiliar insignias. They are also armed, with pistols, which no one here ever is. Their actions are formal, by the book. I am made to stand away from the door, hands out, feet spread apart, while one cautiously chains my wrists and ankles. The other watches with none of the casual, corner-cutting ease daily contact breeds. He is tensed as if I might at any minute snap my bonds and slaughter them both. This thought brings an involuntary smile to my lips. One of our guards would notice, would ask, "What the fuck are you smiling at?" But with these two I have no rapport.

They march me out. It is hard with leg-irons to fall into anything like a rhythm. In addition to acting as a deterrent they are also a clanking metaphor for one's sins, and so doubly shameful.

We follow an unusual path, going back to the administration wing but not by the public route. Some hallways we take seem more like back alleys, barely lit, with an abandoned mop and bucket or a pile of supplies blocking the way. There are no other people.

"What's going on?" I ask.

I am jabbed in the kidney. The baton end plunges deep, causing permanent damage. Systems shut down. Pain is my natural state. I glimpse what it is like to be unprotected by the everyday running of my body. Muscles, bereft of direction, die. The pain of being, that is what a blow to the kidney knocks you into experiencing. All mollifying intentions, words, thoughts, are gone. The only remaining awareness is of life's agony.

"No talking," one of them explains.

It looks bad if you fall. I cannot even console myself imagining them dead, how I would arrange it, with what kind of fitting punishment, so focused am I on not sinking to my knees.

We come to a door. They turn the knob, push it open, but step back. The implication is that I should walk through on my own, which is not so easy. I am still recovering from the aftereffects of the blow.

Heaven, I think. Won't these two creatures be surprised when, after much travail, I am permitted entry and they are not? What a turning of the tables. It enables me to shuffle into the bright carpeted space without falling forward. Heaven, when you know you are going to be pissing blood the next few days, is a heartening prospect.

"Over there," he nods.

They do not come with me. Still shackled, I manage to fit myself into the chair opposite his big desk. I say "his" but that is very much what it is not, anymore. Yes, it is Warden's desk, Warden's office, which we have entered from a private door, but Sweater Man is sitting in the padded swivel chair. In front of him on the desktop lies a half-eaten bagel. It is funny what causes surprise. Mitra's severed head, though spectacular in its way, fit with the general milieu. This place is all about violence, its nuances, how it spills over into aspects of life with which you would not ordinarily expect it to share a common border. But a bagel! I have not seen this particular food in too many years to count. I am rocked. It is still partially wrapped in thick paper, the kind that retains its fold. It is cut in half. Cream cheese is smeared on both faces. I never particularly cared for such an item, would never have gone out of my way to get one when I was free, but now regard it as the center of the universe.

"Good to see you again."

I do not even acknowledge him, so rapt is my devotion. By dipping my head like a farm animal at a trough, I could pick it up and bite off enough to chew, while the rest would fall into my captive hands, which could grasp it tight and defend it against all comers. My torso strains forward.

He resumes eating. He is fastidious, holding on to the paper while attending to the part that sticks out. This is worse than torture. It is indifference. He is just munching away, while still on the job.

"You ditched the sweater," I say, swallowing back saliva.

His mouth is full. I am in danger of crying.

"Last time you were wearing a sweater, and boots. Cowboy boots."

He lifts his leg to show he is still wearing those. Instead of a sweater he has on a shiny black shirt and

those same form-fitting jeans. He chews his bagel and
looks me over.

"Is Warden coming?"

He shakes his head.

He is completely at ease. He has taken over. Yet
all of Warden's knickknacks and awards are still in
evidence. He has just borrowed the office. He finishes
the bagel, pushes the chair back, and looks at me some
more.

"What do you see?" he finally asks.

I frown.

"You're off your medication. That's obvious." He
takes out a handkerchief and wipes his fingers. "For a
while, it looks like."

"No, I'm not."

"So what do you see," he goes on, ignoring my
objection, "now that your brain is back to the way it
was?"

"Nothing."

The shirt is not completely black. Colored thread is
sewn in at the collar and cuffs, wavy lines and curli-
cues. It is what a rodeo cowboy would wear, after
hours. At a fancy function.

"How could you tell?" I ask.

"The whites of your eyes are clear, not scrambled
egg. Your pupils aren't dilated. There are other tells, if
you know where to look."

"Nobody else noticed."

"The people in contact with you every day don't
pick up on changes that are gradual. Are you really
that surprised to see me? Didn't you think I'd be back?"

"—thought maybe the radiation would keep you
from coming."

"The what?"

"The nuclear event."

This, at least, succeeds in wiping the smirk off his face.

"The meltdown," I elaborate. "Why we can't go out into the yard. It's all contaminated. The food too. That explains why you brought that bagel, doesn't it?"

I nod to the wrapping, which still reeks of what it held. I could eat that wax paper in a second. I consider asking him for it.

He seems genuinely shocked.

"You people are . . . It's like you're in Plato's cave or something. You have no idea what's going on, do you? In the world, I mean."

"This is the world."

"You think there's been a nuclear holocaust?"

"Fallout," I correct. "From a power plant meltdown."

"There's no nuclear power plant around here."

"None that you know of."

"What's that supposed to mean?"

"You saying there's no accident? Then how come we're not allowed outside?"

"The prison's been cited for health code violations. A complaint was made by the corrections officers' union. All the exposed wiring and whatnot. They're doing remediation. You know what that is? Cleaning it up." He looks at me, at my unwillingness to be enlightened. "There's no meltdown. Several parts of the facility are off-limits. Including the yard. You're not allowed to go there for your own protection."

"Maybe they wouldn't tell you if there was a meltdown. Ever think of that?"

"So you got your own belief systems and superstitions and everything," he sighs.

"A cave's as real as anything else. I never understood that parable. What makes Plato think the outside is more genuine than the inside? That the guards perceive a higher form of reality than the prisoners?"

"Have you talked to your cellmate?"

"How many times do I have to tell you? He is not my cellmate."

"Soul mate then. Whatever he is. What have you got for me?"

"I don't have anything. I didn't ask to see you."

"Please." He holds up his hand. "Don't go into this whole dumb-man-playing-dumb routine. I'm not Harley. I'm not here to dole out art supplies like some preschool teacher. You got it for me. I know you did. I could tell when we laid it out. You didn't like all that attention he was getting for his book. You didn't like it that he was troubling poor Harley with his lawsuit. You were going to take him down a peg. Show him where the real brains were. That's how you were going to sell it to yourself."

"I didn't find out nothing."

He takes a small rectangle from his pocket and begins tapping the screen.

"I thought devices weren't allowed."

"Who told you that?"

"No one."

He knows! a voice inside me warns. He knows things about yourself that you don't even know! And now he's going to tell you. And after that, you'll be nothing. You'll have no secrets, not even from yourself!

"I found that information you've been wanting."

"What information? I didn't ask you for—"

"About your mother. Yes, I've read your mail." He doesn't bother to look up. "I found out about your mother. Your mother and her 'friend.' "

The walk back to my cell is like a funeral march. The guards actually seem remorseful. The pace at which I am led, how they steady me when I stumble, suggests regret over treating me so harshly on the way in. I am not prodded to indicate a turn. No sudden blow causes the walls of my internal organs to crack and bleed.

What happened in Warden's office is still so troubling that I find it difficult to understand. I had thought giving him the name would be enough.

"Wendy Liu," he confirmed.

"I don't know. Just Wendy."

"What else can you tell me?"

"That's all. The name. That's all you asked."

"The name's usually the last thing that comes up when scum like you and him talk shop."

"I don't like your tone. About my mother—"

"He tell you where she is? This Wendy girl?"

"I don't even know *who* she is. Just that he has nightmares about her. You didn't tell me I had to—"

"Her name was Wendy Liu. Her father's a . . ." He frowns, trying to come up with a word that apparently does not exist. "Her father's got more money than he knows what to do with. One of those. Mostly in China. Although more and more here. His daughter was studying. Is studying. Or so Mr. Liu would like to believe."

"Don't see what that has to do with me."

"You really don't get it, do you? What's been going on."

He took me through my time with Cooney, the game we played at night, showing me what, before, I was unwilling or unable to see: that I had been participating retroactively in his crimes, or crime rather, the one he could not let go of, the one he hugged so close to him all these years.

"No," I objected at first. "That was just us trying to work out our tendencies in a more acceptable way. None of that was about reality. It was guy talk."

"Don't you see how all the options he offered you were the same?"

"I was playing too. I was guiding the scenes in different directions. If I said a certain thing, he accepted that and took it from there."

But when we went over it step by step, image by image, I saw that was not the case. Just as when you try to wheel a defective shopping cart down the aisle and plow into a freestanding display of soup cans, so every collaborative sexual fantasy Cooney and I created veered inexorably toward the same finally quite specific end. He was making me his accomplice after the fact. What I took for an act of mutual consolation was nothing more than my feeding the man's already overdeveloped ego.

"That's not what I intended."

"I don't give a shit what you intended. My job is to find this poor bastard's daughter. What's left of her."

"Who do you work for anyway? What agency?"

"I don't work for the *government*. You think I'd get the results I do if I was a federal employee? Now tell me where she is."

We went over it together. The ending. The inevitable ending. It was—how could I not have seen this?—always the same.

"A ditch. No, not a ditch. He'd correct me when I said that. A culvert. I don't even know what the difference is."

"A culvert goes under something. A road? A highway?"

"How should I know?"

"Don't you understand? You do know."

"Not a road," I grudgingly admitted.

"Why?"

"Because of the sound. There was always a sound that came with it."

"Of what?"

"A train. He was always making a train go by once he stuffed her down there. It would run right over her. 'Here comes that train.' The whistle and everything."

"There's no trains that run through the area she disappeared in."

"Well then maybe you're wrong. Maybe that means he wasn't reliving some—"

"Oh, shit."

He closed his eyes.

"You know it seems to me you're giving him a lot more credit than he deserves."

"Shut up."

I could see him traveling in his mind.

"Twenty miles northwest of Pueblo," he sighed. "The TTC Rail Center for testing tracks. It's a secure facility."

He had been all around where she disappeared. He knew the terrain. Knew the roads. He brought up a map on his device. I was able to narrow the radius down, confirm that the entire encounter happened very quickly, "from meet to greet," as Cooney always put it. Sweater Man must have been devoting considerable time to this. He asked question after question. By the end, he seemed to know exactly where he was heading, and what he would find. Leaning back, he made a few calls. I stared straight ahead at the unattainable wax paper.

At the end, he dropped his relentlessly inquisitory manner and for the first time acted human, treated me almost as an equal, as if we had been through something together.

"What I don't get is, why her? How come this is the only one he didn't brag about in the book?"

It was the first real favor he asked of me, the only question he wasn't sure of getting an answer to. Fittingly, it was the only truth I supplied without hesitation, that I knew for a fact.

"Because she was different." I thought of all his other brides being corn-fed girls from the heartland, the types who usually went for him, and the contempt they brought out. "Because he loved her."

"Love?"

I remembered Cooney's own words, saying how that anthropologist had "introduced her animal soul to love."

Sweater Man gave me a look I am so familiar with. The puzzled pitying look of someone who is himself pathetic, who does not understand the first thing about who we are as creatures, what we are capable of, the expression of a man who has never confronted honest emotion.

As I come down the row, Lanza and one of his goons are unlocking the door to Cooney's cell.

There is a tension between the two sets of guards. Mine, who seem to have overriding authority, are private, as evidenced by their sidearms, their lack of identifying marks. I cannot tell if they are glorified rent-a-cops or part of a shadowy paramilitary organization. Lanza and his underling regard them with suspicion but grudging envy as well.

The rubbing I was working on, my tombstone, still lies on the floor. Relieved of my chains and allowed back into my cell, I go up to the bars and watch.

"What are you doing?"

"Search," Lanza says briefly, to his helper, not me.

He reacts like a dog let off the leash. It is as much about damage as discovery. Lanza stands back, keeping his hands clean.

"Where's Cooney?"

He does not answer.

"You shouldn't be doing that," I call. "Going through his stuff that way. He should be here to witness. He's got documents. Legal documents."

"Can't search a cell with someone in it. You know that."

"Well then where did he go? Where did you take him?"

"I didn't take him anywhere."

"What do you mean?"

"Harms, will you just shut the fuck up?"

"You're violating his civil rights. You should only be searching for contraband. You're not supposed to—"

They have a box and are filling it with various items.

"Holy shit," the assistant says, holding up a piece of cloth.

The nightie sent by the barmaid is not what I would have expected. It is dowdy, almost Victorian; not a silky see-through negligee but flannel, with a homey pattern of flowers, an extra layer to keep him warm. A much more considerate gift, when you think about it.

"—that covered by his constitutional rights?" Lanza asks.

Into the box it goes. I crane my neck but cannot make out what else they are taking.

"He going to get all that back?"

"What do you care?"

It is a good question. I am unnaturally upset, indignant. I am beginning to realize the magnitude of the betrayal I have just committed.

They finish with his possessions and then tip up the mattress. I watch, though I do not expect any great revelation. Cooney is far too smart, prison smart, to have anything that could get him penalized with additional discipline.

"Just making sure you stay within the bounds of the law," I explain while they go through the motions of putting things back together.

"Couple of queers," the other laughs.

This particular flunky's belly hangs over his belt. It is an obvious point of entry. I have been mocked for talking funny ("Look at Harms, with the fifty-dollar words!") but if you examine language it often provides a road map to further action. "Soft underbelly," for example, is not just an expression. It guides the angle of the point. You would be surprised at how resistant bone and cartilage can be to even the most forcefully propelled blade. But if you know the highway, you can travel to where you are going in record speed. I watch his middle-aged body jiggle as he straightens up. Properly directed, a swiftly thrust steak knife could now be surfacing at the back of his throat, tickling the roof of his mouth, while the drench of liberated fluids pours back down in the other direction, through the newly inaugurated canal. My arm, buried in viscera up to its elbow, is smoking hot, wet, engaged.

"Just like it was," Lanza points out, as if I am monitoring in an official capacity.

I suppose I should be concerned for them as well, these upholders of civic virtue. They are far more brutalized than those of us ground under their boot soles each day. They are still on a downward trajectory. They have not bottomed out as we have, are not languishing in sin or beginning their slow painful climb. With every shift they take a few more steps toward damnation.

The cell is left so shoddily reconstructed there is little doubt what has taken place. Cooney will be furious when he returns. I lie on my bed and stare. The hopelessness I struggle to keep at bay comes right up and sniffs me. I do not realize then, nor will I for several more days, the significance of what has just happened, that Cooney will never return, that he is gone, disappeared, without a word of explanation, with barely an acknowledgment that he ever existed. And I do not allow myself to see, for an even longer time, that it is my doing.

10.

"Where did they take his stuff to?" I ask Mbaéré, who has been pressed into service manning the cart.

I can tell he is not happy at the assignment, either because of the disrespect implied by such a demotion or the prospect of meeting the same fate as Mitra.

"His personal effects, I mean. Lanza and some other guards took them away that day. Do you know if they were sent on to another location?"

He pretends not to hear.

"What about his medications?" I persist. "Do you have a cup with his name on it? Cooney 751113?"

"Who?"

"Is he in the Sick Unit?"

"I have no idea whom you are speaking of."

He stares significantly. His eyes are even more bloodshot than usual. He is shivering inside an over-size woolen coat.

"They *transfer* him?"

"Harms, please take your dosage. The cold out here is killing."

It must be that thin, sub-Saharan blood, I theorize, swallowing and simultaneously summoning a mighty cough which propels the medication to its hiding place behind my eyes. My pupils locate individual pills as they interfere with the functioning of each optic nerve. It is an exquisite irritation.

"Trays!" he calls, about to move on.

"Wait."

He turns and regards me with something like concern. It is confusing to see such an attitude from anyone in this place. I forget what I am about to say.

"How are you feeling?" he asks.

"What do you think? Been cooped up in here forever, with the repairs."

"It is a difficult time for all of us."

Now I remember why I detained him.

"During an interrogation, you said a person wouldn't give up information unless he truly wanted to."

"Did I?"

"But why? What would make him want to rat out his friends?"

"Compliance," he says. "The desire to comply with another's expectations is very strong. Particularly with someone in a position of authority."

"I need to know where Cooney is. There's questions I was going to ask him. Things he was going to tell me. I have to understand why—"

"Trays!" he calls, the cart squeaking as he turns.

The itch becomes unmanageable. Trying not to rip my eyes out, I clutch the bowl. The smooth porcelain is my friend. I sneeze and snort and shudder whatever is inside me until it shakes loose. The bumps, now with a strange jellied coating, plop onto the surface. "I'm melting!" they scream, little Wicked Witches of the West, impediments to my spiritual growth. I spit on them.

Nothing happens here for so long a time, and minuscule uninteresting events are so blown out of proportion, that when actual news occurs, a truly significant development, it is often met with a surprisingly blasé response. I do not know if this is because it is so grand it fails to register on our diminished scale of perception or because like all creatures we wish to play it cool and pretend we are not susceptible to outside influence. Thus the disappearance of Cooney is met with a collective shrug. His cell sits empty, which is itself unusual as there is serious overcrowding. A unit rarely remains vacant. The off-center mattress and depleted cardboard file boxes take on an air of disheveled permanence, the new normal.

No one will talk about it. I try engaging people in conversation and meet a stubborn resistance. It is almost as if the presence of an unseen third party looms, the same power that whisked him away still being capable of wreaking havoc on anyone who speaks its name.

Dinner, a misnomer right from the start as it takes place at four forty-five, is a dismal affair. One lines up with one's plastic plate and is served slop from a bubbling cauldron. I am barely conscious, so routine and disappointing is the experience, and do not notice until the last moment whom I am facing.

"You?" I ask, involuntarily sounding a note of wonder.

Littlejohn is standing before me with a ladle. I shake off my lethargy and try not to gape.

"Plate," he says.

"How did you get this job?"

I confirm he is really in charge of dispensing the main course. It is a privilege inmates spend years plotting to be awarded. There is more time out of your cell, human contact, an actual task to be performed, and something akin to private dining, being allowed to eat first when the cafeteria is practically empty. It is inconceivable that such a recent resident could ever score this prize assignment.

He nods again to the plate. I hand it over and watch him dispense a not particularly generous portion of chipped beef over dry bread. The gastronomic name for this dish is Creamed Foreskins on Toast.

"How did you manage to swing this?" I persist.

There are several lines and we are shielded from the guards, so I manage to stand off to one side and engage him in conversation while he, captive audience, continues to dish out.

"What do you mean?"

"This job. What did you have to do?"

"I didn't have to do anything. One of them just took me out early."

"One of the guards? Which?"

"I don't know."

His shoulders slope. His body, even performing this menial task, still showcases its animal ease.

"He didn't ask for anything in return?"

We both look to see if anyone is listening, but food, even inedible institutional fare, creates an overwhelming anticipatory effect. People receive their bounty and go off to stuff themselves.

"Nobody just gets this gig," I whisper. "People fight for it. Hell, people *fuck* for it."

"I didn't do shit," he frowns. "He just took me here and said what to do."

"Who?"

"I told you, I don't know. I don't know their names."

"So it's not him then? The one who's doing it to you?"

I stare at his chest, where the bruises I saw in the shower must still bloom.

"No!"

"Then who is?"

He pretends to focus on centering a particular ladleful just right.

"Even if it's a guard, there's things we can do. Guards are not immune. They can be subject to discipline. If you don't want to go to the authorities, I can—"

"Will you just leave me alone?"

"I can save you," I insist. "I can guide you back to the right path."

Just for an instant an expression of helplessness appears on his face. This is how he must be, I sense, when alone with his tormentor, a marionette with all its strings cut, a passive figure saying, "Do with me what you will."

"But you have to ask forgiveness."

There is a bit of impatience. My distracting him has slowed the line's progress. Moments in this place are dictated by circumstance. I see tears in his formerly dead gaze, just two, welling, a first tentative attempt to bring life back to that parched stare.

"What's even harder, you have to forgive yourself."

A guard is approaching to see what the problem is. Reluctantly, I grip my tray and walk off. Once again I have planted a seed. Now it is up to him.

Forgive yourself because without learning to use that primitive moral muscle the forgiving of others is not possible. That is one of the reasons we are here, because we judge ourselves so harshly. So-called normal people commit grievous offenses and continue on through their lives as if nothing has happened. They do not see, in black and white, how irrevocably lost their souls are. Our seriousness does not permit such an existence, one of compromise and degree. With no forgiveness to lavish upon ourselves, the notion of "feeling" what others supposedly "feel" is obscene.

Forgive yourself if you can, I ruefully amend, wedging myself into an empty spot at a table, knowing how hard this first and, in some sense, only step is. As the saying goes, "Forgive and forget." It is a form of extinction, to extend love to the monster we have worked so hard to create. Once we do, the monster ceases to exist, and then . . . what takes its place?

Meals are taken at cafeteria-style tables that have benches bolted underneath. I find myself sitting opposite Shelburne, who seems unfazed by the steaming mass of cornstarch and animal renderings before him. He gobbles it up as if we are at a five-star eatery.

"No wonder he stopped coming here."

I take a bite, reacquaint myself with the peculiarly grainy texture of reconstituted beef flakes.

"Who?" Shelburne asks.

I was not even aware I was speaking out loud.

"Cooney." Emboldened by the perceptible change in the rhythm of plastic utensils scraping on plates, I go on: "I'm just saying it makes sense, Cooney getting those boxed meals. Whatever was inside them had to be better than this."

He tears a little of his bread to smear up sauce.

"You don't think it's peculiar, his cell staying empty? I mean, how long's he been gone now? Two, three weeks?"

There is never much conversation at these affairs, but the ensuing silence is notable even by ordinary standards.

Why care? I ask myself, echoing Lanza's observation. It is dangerous to care, an unwise investment unless you are fairly sure of getting something in return; protection, sympathy, a reduction of longing . . . all of which I did receive from Cooney, all of which I feel the lack of now that he is away.

"How long before they usually fill a bed? A few days, at most. But this . . . It's like they erased who he was, so now they can't take advantage of the space he left behind. Because that would *prove* something."

"Shouldn't take what don't belong to you," Shelburne unexpectedly volunteers.

It sounds awkward, almost rehearsed.

"What are you talking about?"

"I'm saying if you don't make it right, I'm going to have to dock me some balls."

"That so? All by your lonesome?"

I try to silently remind him how he reacted when that botched victim of his came crawling out of her poorly dug grave and sent him running onto the highway, straight into the lights of a state trooper vehicle.

"Just give it back."

"I have no idea what you're referring to."

"Won't be any fuss. No questions asked."

"I thought we were talking about Raymond Cooney."

"Shut the fuck up," someone suggests from down the row.

"Just what the hell did I do to piss you off?"

"Not me. I don't give a shit."

"Then who?"

He swallows. Or tries to. He is not supposed to be telling but is egged on by knowing something I do not, by having the chance to show off.

"—said it took him a month, getting it right."

"Who? Who said that?"

He coughs.

"Getting what right?"

He drops his spoon and half-rises from the bench, hands searching the area above his sternum.

"You OK?"

"Asshole," someone comments, bestowing the word generally, like fairy dust.

I suppose it does have a universal application.

Shelburne's hands flutter. His face changes. Again there is a shift in the rhythm of utensils on plates but no one actually stops, which is understandable. It's not like you can take your leftovers home in a doggie bag.

"Need a little help here!" I call.

The guards, when I try to get their attention, only squint.

"Got a man choking!"

His hands tear apart his shirt. There is nothing of use beneath, no trap door, no way in. His eyes are swelling, bloating beyond the dimensions of their sockets.

. . . some kind of "maneuver," my mind idly recalls, where you squeeze a person's chest. I read a description once. Saw pictures. What was it? A funny name.

Those eyes are bulging but also focused, not on me, even though I am sitting directly across from him. Shelburne looks past me, his expression one of terror and pleading. I turn.

"Fucking bones," someone else complains.

The next row over, staring back at him, is Stanley. His eyes emit a steady, unblinking command. Shelburne gives up on ripping open his throat. He claws at his jaw, tries reaching down, exposes crooked teeth, creates a ghastly, inappropriate grin.

Heimlich Maneuver! I triumphantly recall, and with that odd name comes a vision of the accompanying illustration.

I climb up on the tabletop. It would take too long to extricate myself the conventional way and run all around to the other side. I crawl across the surface, scattering plates, ignoring curses and slow-motion drug-numbed indignation.

This, not a man choking to death right in front of them, but my leaving my seat without permission, gets the guards' attention. Several whistles blow at once.

I slide down the other side. By now, Shelburne is slumped on the table. His body is quivering. I approach from behind and lock my fists under his ribcage. He weighs a ton. I lift several times. Nothing happens. It is like trying to shift a boulder. I look up and see Stanley, still beaming his unadulterated poison right into Shel's brain. He is rocking slightly, excited, murdering him by suggestion. I note the telltale stream of drool dribbling onto his pants. Readjusting my grip, I give a sharp yank.

"Oh!" Shelburne exclaims, not the word itself, but air propelling the blockage out his windpipe, sending a spray of food particles across the table.

He coughs, then sucks back in a long noisy bucket of oxygen. It goes on forever, one breath.

"Where is Raymond Cooney?" I demand.

A hand grabs my shoulder and spins me around.
Several batons hit me at once.

Dear Mother,

*I write to you from the "Holding Cell," though it is nei-
ther nurturing nor supportive. More commonly referred to
as the Rubber Room, this is where inmates who have been
pacified are put to make sure they do not harm themselves or
others. The unit lacks such usual amenities as bars or lights.
The furnishings do not include what one would laughingly
call essentials; a bed, say, or the proverbial pot to piss in.
Instead there is a small, cunningly designed latrine-like hole
with a faded artist's rendering of where to place one's hind-
quarters. As for sleep, a blanket is my bed. I take it wherever
I wish within the five- or perhaps seven-foot-square area. It
is impossible to measure with any degree of accuracy, there
being only an eerie, indirect illumination that never goes
quite on or off, playing tricks with one's perception.*

*I have, of course, no writing implements, no paper, no
desk, so am forced to rely on my powers of psychic transmit-
tal. I hope this reaches you, as what I have to say is urgent
and, as the expression goes, "time sensitive."*

*But first, who is Mrs. Josephine Hallquist and why are
you now residing at her legal address? I am informed (please
don't ask by what means) that the said "Mrs." is a divorced
woman with no visible means of support except a rather
significant savings account. How did you meet her, if you
don't mind my asking? Are you contributing to the upkeep
of the establishment? It also has come to my attention, not
by asking but because of an overzealous acquaintance with
perhaps too much incentive, that your barmaiding and waitressing days are now a thing of the past! Apparently you
and this Mrs. Hallquist are cohabitating, with neither of*

you showing much interest in the external world besides the occasional foray to the supermarket or liquor store. I hope you won't think it forward of me if I ask just what this "love nest" you seem to be feathering for yourself is all about? And why have you failed to notify the post office of your new status? Are you aware that my letters are returned with a stamp calling your whereabouts UNKNOWN? At least this communication, the one I am directing to you with all my mental might, will not be so easily deflected.

Of course what you do with your own life is, as has always been the case, a private matter. Lately it has become apparent to me that I was never more than a hindrance, an obstruction, on your road to . . . where I could never quite figure out. (The place you are in now, I suppose, some perverted safe haven of "happiness" I am denied even knowledge of, much less entry to.) I realize I am a source of guilt— shame, even—negatively affecting your standing in the community, but still think I deserve the courtesy of an occasional progress report, a "kind word." I certainly have provided you with enough of those over the years, hellish though my own circumstances may have been.

And they are hardly better now, if you must know the truth, which is why I have chosen to go to the extreme length of speaking to you through this unusual channel. Do not be alarmed. I am not "there," inside you. You are no more responsible for my actions now than you were during that trying time when so many people tried to drive a wedge between us. (Neither are you any less responsible, I might add, but that is a conversation for a different day.) I am simply the voice of your conscience suggesting that your son, your only child, is in difficulty, grave even by his standards, and that he could use some solace, some warmth, such as that supplied by a few heartfelt sentiments written out in your own personal penmanship. DO NOT USE A PRINTER which I imagine someone like Mrs. Hallquist possesses. That would ruin everything. What I miss is your touch, even if it is simply the amount of pressure you exert on a ballpoint pen. I am sensitive to such things, as you no doubt remember. It used to give you pleasure, my sensitivity. When did that stop? I suppose Mrs. Hallquist is introducing you to all sorts of new things. Perhaps she has a "color" TV, as well. All I can offer, by way of an alternative, is our shared past and the good times we had, which I realize is not enough, but is not nothing either. In any event, please do drop me a line, by the mundane medium of the US mails. I thank you in advance.

As for what I am doing here, besides suffering: I am the victim of a wide-ranging conspiracy which deliberately misinterpreted an action of mine (a positive action, saving a man's life) as an assault, as being "aggressive." This was not an isolated incident. I have felt, over the last few weeks, a distance yawn between myself and the rest of the world, wider, deeper, even, than the usual chasm. I do not know what set it off. Stress? Well, there is always stress in one's life. The question is how you deal with it. I recently suffered a loss. (Yes, even here, where one has nothing, one can still be bereft.) Perhaps that was the straw that broke the camel's back. In addition, I have lately felt that my ministry, my mission to save others in this gloomy place, has seen its progress stall. I can steer the conversation around to guilt and responsibility, repentance and redemption, but coarse concerns—physical comfort, loneliness, the exercising of one's nature—blot out so many of the higher feelings. I am as guilty of this backsliding as everyone else. The fault, as always, is mine. Indeed, I sometimes feel that if I could only live a blameless life, here, in this concentrated cesspool of humanity's flaws, this society stripped of delusion, if I

*could simply (!) transform myself into a shining beacon, I
could save them all, the whole human race, lead us to a hum-
bler cleaner form of existence. Then you would be proud of
me; then, perhaps, you would let me know where you truly
reside.*

I am laughing as I compose this. I am keeping my
teeth ground shut but the laughter spills all around
them the way floodwater spurts up through a cellar
door, a high, whinnied giggling. The Rubber Room.
There is no rubber here. You bounce off the walls at
your peril. Worst is the light. Is it smoky and viscous
by nature or is this a permanent hangover from the fire
they pumped directly into my vein? One arm is still
weak at the point of entry. The needle was the kind
they use to blow up basketballs or bicycle tires. I push
the photons aside. Slowly they reassert, like sludge.

"It was Stanley!" I call, less in hope of engendering
a response than to try and get an acoustic map of the
room.

The walls and not-wall share so many characteris-
tics. I keep bumping into a border, but it is not continuous, does not form a coherent shape. There are voids. I
fall, hit myself, fall again, come to rest, lie panting. The
lumbar region of my back throbs. My lungs lap up the
soot suspension that passes for air.

"There are no bones in Creamed Foreskins on
Toast," I explain. "Stanley was controlling him mentally. Shelburne was running at the mouth. He was
about to tell me something. Stanley had to shut him
up."

Names and faces float past, storm-borne debris. All
I remember clearly is the burning acid establishing a

base camp in my bicep before fanning out and searing every nook and cranny of my brain.

"Shhh," a voice counsels. "You're hurting yourself."

I grope toward the sound. A hand, lazily, with a caress doubling as a shove, drives me back down, stops me from causing further damage by inflicting pain of its own.

"Poor Ethan," it murmurs. "Are you hungry?"

My heart leaps at what the hands now produce. Grapes! Store-bought, old, perhaps a little brown and withered, but the most purely preserved taste of sun and earth there is. What he introduced me to, so many years ago. The sensual world.

"Are you sure I'm allowed?"

"Go ahead."

With trembling care, I detach one and place it on my tongue. I crush it, then begin to chew ferociously.

"Slow down."

He puts his hand on my head, trying to calm febrile thoughts, stanch my tears.

"Relax."

"Easy for you to say." I almost choke. "I've been waiting all my life for this."

"Don't be so dramatic."

His hand does not let go. His fingers are soothing the top of my skull. They check the condition of various bumps and depressions, map the essential me underneath. It is not like when Warden touches me. Warden paws. These fingers are sure. They form my abnormalities rather than seek them out.

"What are you doing here, Father?"

"You asked for me. Don't you remember?"

I shake my head. The fingers pry deeper.

"Apparently you had some kind of accident. A seizure. You've been sedated, for your own protection. You kept asking to see me. I was as surprised as anyone when the prison authorities tracked me down. They must do quite a bit of background work on their inmates."

"I'm a special case. I've been useful to them."

"You were always useful, Ethan."

"They were afraid of what I'd say."

"Eat."

"How come you're not having any?"

He laughs quietly.

"What's so funny?"

"This is hell."

He says it as one intimate with the place. But hell is not an actual locale, I reason. It can be anywhere.

"I live in Tulsa now. I've started a youth ministry there."

"I thought you were suspended. Or, what's the expression, 'Relieved of your pastoral duties?' "

"A bunch of false accusations I'm dealing with. I still perform all my routine duties. I just can't celebrate Mass."

"That's a shame."

"What did you do to your face?"

"I didn't do anything. It was them."

I can feel his gaze, even here in the half-light, taking a keen inventory of my cuts and bruises. I try returning the favor, look at him directly. Father Bryan has not lacked for nourishment in the years since we last met. His outfit's basic black limits the visual calamity somewhat, but the overall impression is that of an allegorical portrait: Gluttony Crossed with Lust. His eyes are buttons buried deep in an upholstered chair.

"They said you wanted to see me because you thought you were about to be executed. Do you remember that?"

"No."

There are no more grapes. I keep going, eat the stems, the bits of woody vine.

"You're not going to tell anyone, are you?"

"Is that why you came?"

"I came because you asked me to."

"You never came before."

"I thought you wouldn't want to see me. That maybe you thought I was to blame."

"For what I did? Don't be silly." I force myself to slow down. Soon there will be nothing left. "I don't blame other people."

"Maybe you should."

"That would dilute my achievement."

I see he has no idea what I am talking about. A fugitive memory of our time together forces me to smile.

"You got a helper," I ask, "in your ministry?"

"What makes you think that?"

"Can't have a youth ministry without a youth."

"They said you were making all kinds of accusations. Unfounded claims, they called them."

"But not about you."

"Then why did you ask for me?"

"I guess I felt the need to unburden my soul."

"Don't!" he says quickly, looking all around.

"They're not listening. Besides, anything we say is confidential."

"Not anymore. Didn't you hear me? I'm not authorized. I can't administer any of the sacraments. Including confession."

"So who is he?"

The features, from within their blubber, dismiss this suggestion.

"Ernie? Jack?" I tease. "Come on, Father, who's your new friend? Skip?"

"Please." He bats his eyelashes. "You think his name would be Skip?"

That coquetry I found so anomalous, so intriguing, there is still a whiff of it left, like the sunshine in my mouth from the last rotting greenhouse grape.

"I think my mother has become a lesbian. Is that possible?"

"Your mother's had a tough time."

"And I haven't?"

"You can't say anything, Ethan. I'm hanging on by my fingernails. I can't have any more associations being raised, especially with a case like yours. If they found out about us that would pretty much be the end of it for me."

"Then why did you come?"

"Feelings?" he shrugs.

"I want to confess."

"No," he whispers, coming close. "You've got to keep it all to yourself. Understand?"

11.

"—fry *platter*," he insists.

I summon Eldridge (knowing he is dead) the way you look up an old friend. His tale of last meals haunts me. I try remembering what we actually had the night before he died, his true last supper, but it has sunk back into the general morass of time served.

"And who betrayed you?" I wonder.

"What?"

"Nothing."

I have been back in my cell three days now. Three days during which I am supposed to "re-acclimate," meaning have no contact with the general population. In such situations it does not matter whom you talk to, the definitely deceased as opposed to the so-called living. More important is what they say, what you prompt them into revealing about your own mind. The only way to avoid *going* crazy is to get to crazy first, so any direction you take from there will be *out*. Does that make sense?

"Not to me," he says good-naturedly.

That was always Eldridge's strong suit. A geniality. Whether deflecting questions about his dismemberment of a family of five or recounting with mouthwatering accuracy his pre-electric-chair fare he always had a sense of optimism and humor.

"Fry platter then," I amend. "But if you had to do it over—"

"Enchiladas." He is surprisingly certain. "And a pitcher of cold beer."

"Beer? They're not going to let you have alcohol in jail. Not even on your last night."

"What the fuck," he shrugs, in his invisible, disembodied way.

"Anyway that's not what I meant. I was going to ask if you had to do your *life* over, or resume it, rather, if you could walk out of here on your own two legs, not have your vital essence swirl down the shower drain like it did, but find yourself free, by virtue of some god-sent miracle, what would you do?"

"Don't need to do nothing," he advises. "Just stay where you are. Let the game come to you."

"What game? What are you talking about?"

But he is no longer here. Our connection has gone dead.

Enchiladas, I consider. A boring choice.

"What about something more exotic?" I call out, hoping he will return. "Maybe chicken in a molé sauce?"

"Harms."

Harris and another guard are standing in front of my cell.

"You have a visitor."

"Me?"

After time in the Rubber Room, I assumed all my privileges would be suspended for at least a month.

"Sit," he orders, pointing rather needlessly with his baton.

"Why? Aren't we going to—?"

He motions again with his little stick. I am sure times are tough outside, that jobs are scarce, but I still do not see why anyone would willingly choose to be a prison guard. It seems such an admission of defeat, that you compensate for all your failings and deficiencies by lording it over men of far greater accomplishment, those whose only crime is running afoul of society's squeamish contradictory mores. The way guards swagger, their absurd augmentations of power, truncheons, plastic handcuffs, chuckling radios, clearly mark them as men not gifted with any natural attributes.

"And those little tacos," Eldridge adds, reappearing as I sit back down on the edge of my bed. "Bite-size. *Ta-qui-tos*."

They open the door. Harris comes in while the younger one hangs back. He looks all around as if there might be some bogeyman poised to leap out from an equally nonexistent closet.

"What's it all about?" I ask.

"Change in procedure."

"Since when?"

"Since you been away."

He nods to his partner, who signals down the row. "Interrogation rooms are off-limits now. Asbestos removal. You're going to have a supervised visit in your cell. If you have any physical contact with the visitor, or even approach the visitor, we're going to terminate the session."

Someone is making their way down the corridor, inciting a cascade of catcalls from the gallery.

"Why don't you just chain me up?" I suggest, "if you're so afraid I'll misbehave?"

"That's what we usually do now, but she said no."

He settles his bulk on the toilet seat. There is an audible groan. I feel a pang of sympathy for the porcelain.

"You're staying?"

"I told you, it's a supervised visit. I am going to be in the cell, at all times," he recites, quoting from a memo.

Dr. Roberta Bush comes into view. She is walking stiff-legged, pretending to be oblivious to the hormonal hackles being raised at her presence. Womanhood is met with a mix of worship and anger in the cell block.

The air echoes with orangutan hoots, attempts to engage in dialogue, as well as colorfully expressed non sequiturs. I admire how she ignores it all. I suppose it is just a grotesque exaggeration of what any woman encounters walking down Main Street, USA.

"Ethan," she says, looking around. "So this is where you live."

"You shouldn't have come."

I gaze significantly at our unwanted third party, this hulking interloper who appears to have dropped by to take a dump.

"Is it really necessary for you to be here?"

"Yes, ma'am."

"Mr. Harms and I have spent many hours in conversation. Alone."

"It's for your own protection."

I am conflicted. I want to get up, both as a sign of respect and to have her use the bed as her seat while I stand. But I am afraid it will be interpreted as an attempt at "physical contact" and so provide Harris and his friend an excuse to cancel our interview before it even starts, not to mention inflict a clumsy assault on me after she leaves.

"I can't do my work under these conditions."

He shrugs.

"All right," she smiles.

I see her mind functioning. She senses they want her to call the interview off, which only strengthens her resolve. She is one of those women who comes into her own when challenged. Does Seth do that? I wonder. Stand up to her? Bring out the jaw-jut and stubborn defiance she is exhibiting now? I doubt it.

She sits on the floor. She is wearing a skirt, a long-ish one, but still a risky fashion choice in a house of detention. She folds her legs and it rides up. I watch her take out the familiar notebook, folder, pens, and then something new, an object I cannot identify.

"Never seen the top of your head," I offer.

I mean it as a pleasantry, a joke, referring to my, for once, sitting higher than her. But it comes out all creepy.

"Well, I've never seen your shoes," she counters.

I have a moment of panic. Do my feet smell? Could I have stepped in something? There are disgusting things here. Overflows. Bubblings-up. But then I realize she, too, is nervous. There is a first date awkward-ness to our encounter, as well as something absurdly funny. We both grin.

"How are the nuptials?"

"The what?"

"Your wedding plans."

She hesitates. It is against the rules, but somehow our being here, in uncharted previously forbidden ter-ritory, makes it OK to be a little less formal. We feel a bond, presenting a united front against these eaves-droppers, these goons who pretend not to pay atten-tion to every word we speak. They are the prisoners, I want to assure her, shackled by their petty, conven-tional minds.

"We rented a space. There's not going to be a cer-emony so we're going directly from the county clerk's office to the Marriott."

"Marriott?" I frown.

She is amused.

"It's not as cheesy as it sounds. They have a very nice banqueting hall. We're spending a lot on flowers. I like . . . flowers."

Perhaps she decides that is going too far. For my part, I am doing my best not to squirm. I miss the restraints, the way I would test myself against them, feel the reassuring bite of steel. Muscles have memories, just like the heart. And just like those more highly prized recollections, they come unbidden, are hard to dismiss.

"You'll be a beautiful bride."

"We were talking about Anne Greenaway."

She flips through her notebook as if to check on exactly where we left off. I *can* see the top of her head. I said it just to fill the silence but like most remarks you drop in passing it turns out to be a profound observation. Her hair is parted down the middle. It is dark, so there is a white canal, a line running down the center leading to—I remember from an old anatomy textbook liberated from the upper shelves—that soft spot dead-center at the top of the skull. In a baby it is still mushy. The skull turns out not to be all of a piece. It is composed of panels coming together around a void, the fontanel. After a few weeks, they fuse and close up, but never completely. There is still a little escape hatch at the very top of who you are. And, like all escape hatches, it is also a way in.

"You remember?" she prompts.

"I do. But I can't—"

My eyes indicate Harris. She gives him a rapid, dismissive stare.

"You've already been found guilty of your crimes, Ethan. You can't incriminate yourself further by discussing them."

" —wouldn't be right."

"Maybe it would. Maybe it would demystify the whole event for you, describing it matter-of-factly in front of someone you don't care about."

"I care about everyone."

"Even Anne Greenaway?"

"Her especially."

"We're not going to have that fight again, are we?"

"Where are you going on your honeymoon?"

She picks up the object she has brought. It is a flat leather case, with a hinge. She parts it in two, revealing a photo holder, the kind you prop on a dresser or table. She holds it out like I am supposed to start crying.

"This is Anne at seventeen."

I nod.

"The other one's Kate Imbriano. Remember her?"

"This is disappointing," I sigh. "That you would stoop so low."

"Me?"

"This is something I would expect from a TV reporter, like when they shove a microphone in your face."

Nevertheless, I am aware of my fingers digging down into the mattress.

"I have more photos. I have photos of all of them."

"Why are you only showing me two, then? And why are they in that contraption?"

"I thought we could go over them two at a time. In order."

"Ah, chronology, the hobgoblin of little minds."

She sets it up like this is a room! In a house! Sometimes the smallest assumption lays bare how monstrously far apart two people can be, even those who care for each other.

"Excuse me," I say to Harris. "Will you please stop staring at my guest's legs?"

"He bothering you?" Harris asks.

She ignores him.

"I thought dealing with them in pairs might break up this logjam you seem to have in confronting what you did. Make it more manageable, bring out similarities, a pattern, even, that you hadn't thought of yourself."

"Oh, she is ripe for the taking," Eldridge cackles.

"Shut up."

"What?"

I actually feel him slap my thigh. It takes all my inner strength not to respond.

"Roberta," I say. "May I call you that?"

Harris shifts uncomfortably. I am going to be constipated for a week, terrified of what I might pick up, even through his government-issued trousers. They say you can't get things from toilet seats, but two-hundred-fifty-plus pounds of porcine ignorance leaves its residue on any surface.

"What I did was entered into evidence at my trial. They had expert witnesses explaining what happened. They had pictures. They had detectives. You don't need me to go over all that again. I have nothing to add. Besides it's like asking a chicken how he lays eggs. He doesn't know. He just does it."

"She. A chicken laying eggs is a she."

"Well, then it's like how a bear shits in the woods. Does that work better for you?"

She pulls her skirt down. It goes right back up again.

I do not trust myself to do more than nod at the diptych, because that, of course, is what it is, some churchy attempt to immortalize. My hands are locked in the mattress, the way a cat gets its claws stuck in a carpet.

"You come here and try and get a rise out of me. I don't know what for. For your own amusement, I think. Not for any PhD thesis."

"There's been violence in my family, in my past. I'm trying to understand it."

"There's violence everywhere. It's what this place is built on. You think studying it in some pure form is going to help you make sense of things?"

"I need to *know*."

I feel another spell coming.

"You mess with my head when I've already been—" I stop, trying to master the shakes. "At least here they punish you for a reason. Compared to the outside world this is beginning to feel like the last bastion of sanity."

"Hawaii," she offers.

"What?"

"That's where we're going on our honeymoon."

"You don't have money for a real gold ring or a nicer place than a Marriott, but you're flying all the way to Hawaii?"

"Seth has a relative who— Wait." She turns to the guard. "I'm going to have to insist that you stand outside with your colleague. I have a note saying I am to be granted *private access* to the prisoner."

I think it is her use of the word "colleague," ennobling him to that extent, or maybe it is the skirt riding up, a strange and unexpected exercise of power. He shifts on his seat, confused.

"Lady, are you sure?"

She continues to stare.

He heaves his bulk off the porcelain and walks out of the cell. It is only a few steps, but he no longer exists.

"Listen," she says in a barely audible tone, urgent and direct. "If you have anything to tell me, now's the time."

"I have plenty of things to tell you, just not about—"

"This is our last meeting, Ethan. I won't be able to schedule any more."

"Because of your marriage?"

"No! My marriage changes nothing in terms of our work. The authorities here have gotten very difficult about allowing access. I had to call six times before they said yes and that was only under the condition that I just conduct a short exit interview, wrapping things up for my study."

"Maybe they know best."

"What's that supposed to mean?"

"What good can come of this?"

She reaches into her blouse and produces a small slip of paper.

They cannot see, because her back is to them. They cannot see, because I keep an absolutely straight face, betray no sign as our hands, which she deliberately makes meet, entangle briefly, something between a caress and a tussle, during which the information is transferred. I was not even aware of my fingers, previously tensed, fixed in rigid curves, transforming themselves to messengers of emotion. Now they are pliable, so permeated with feeling they have trouble closing around the clandestine bit of writing.

"It's my address. If you send the letters to 'Mrs. R. Lowenstein,' it shouldn't be a problem. They won't make the connection."

"What am I supposed to write?"

"You know what." She is once again the tough, no bullshit woman warrior, the one who hides behind nail polish and academic jargon. "Write me when you're ready to tell me what you did. Step by step. Every crime. I'm going to get it out of you. Until there's nothing left."

"They read outgoing mail."

"I'm sure you can find a way to tell me without them knowing." She spreads her legs in preparation for getting off the floor. Her skirt rides up until it is no longer a skirt. This is definitely not an accident. She lingers long enough to ensure getting my attention. "We have our own language, don't we?"

I do not answer. I do not have to. Which is proof we do, I suppose.

She reaches past me to retrieve the framed portraits. The space between her arm and chest sends a wave of warmth, of sweat, of personal odor so strong that all I want in the world is to be a molecule on her skin. Then she is gone, with no further words. No good-bye. I hear her bantering with the guards on her way up the row, that tone reserved for talk with fellow outsiders, for the 99.9 percent of encounters that make up her life. I strain my ears to hear what they are discussing but it is incomprehensible, a mode of communication I once knew, now long forgotten.

"You're amazingly untalented," Warden says.

Why am I offended? I never claimed to know what I was doing. This whole elaborate ruse was his idea. He indicated that if I brought my materials, claimed to be drawing his portrait, it would deflect attention from the true purpose of our meeting. Yet he laughs at the results. I want to assault him.

"It's more a record of my thoughts."

"That supposed to make me feel better?"

"I didn't come here to make you—"

I check myself. His authority may be diminished but just because of that the power he does retain is even more precious to him.

He has dark circles around his eyes. I do not know what to do with them. Initially I draw black rings, but they make him look silly. I try smudging them, which turns him bleary and weak.

"You can drop the pose, Ethan. I didn't expect to end up with a likeness suitable for framing."

"I enjoy this." My hands are filthy. When they try steadying the paper, which I have propped on the back of a plaque he allowed me to remove from the wall, they leave fingerprints. "Makes it easier to talk."

He waits expectantly.

"So are you going to do anything about it?" I ask.

"Not sure what you think I'm supposed to do. You claim this inmate is being physically tortured by a guard?"

"Abused. Not just a beatdown. It's more systematic than that."

"But you don't know who. Which guard. And then you're hinting that it might be *consensual*?"

"Nothing's consensual here."

"You'll get no argument from me about that. But there's procedure. Protocol. I can't just swoop down and make things right."

"Seems like that's what happened before. Not with you but that other guy. He didn't let procedure get in his way."

The more I draw, the further away he gets. I am obscuring, rather than revealing. Is that true of all art? I wonder. Is it really just a way of not seeing?

"He isn't coming this time, in case you're wondering."

"Who?"

"The gentleman you just referred to."

"I didn't expect to see him again. He got what he wanted out of me."

"Yes, he did. And we're—I'm—eternally grateful."

"Why? What did I do for you?"

"Are you kidding? That lawsuit Cooney was filing, that production company trying to get in here to film, those reporters bugging me for interviews? All gone." He waves his fingers. "Like magic."

"Cooney too. Gone. Like magic."

You would think all this leaves him happy, but he is the opposite. I keep looking up and down, at him and at the drawing. He is sinking deeper and deeper into his fate. It is not just the eyes. His body is tensed and vulnerable, diminished, as if it has lost some inner strength.

"I couldn't help that," he frowns. "It was the price to pay."

The likeness is growing more depressing. I give up, feeling I am in some way responsible.

"So you have no idea where Cooney is?"

He fiddles with the objects on his desk.

"This Wendy Liu, the girl I told that man about, her father's a pretty big deal, huh?"

"You have no idea."

"Big enough to snatch a man out of federal prison? Make it seem like he was never here to begin with?"

"Bigger than that. Big enough to make all those other people go away too. Anyone who might make a stink."

"How'd he manage that?"

"How do you think? Money. All those newspapers and law firms and movie studios, they're corporations. They all get down on their hands and knees and kiss up to the almighty buck."

"I don't."

"That's because you have the luxury of being incarcerated."

I set the botched drawing aside. The plaque proclaims him Association of Correctional Administrators Man of the Year. Almost a decade ago.

"So you have no idea where Cooney's got to?"

"The whole world is in flux these days. Can't pin a person down to one specific spot anymore. Would you mind being more careful? That's a very prestigious award."

I am compulsively scratching at the surface, as if I could remove the incised lettering, or add a comment of my own.

"Everything's back to normal, huh?"

He avoids my gaze, which is a switch. Some balance of power has shifted. I do not like it. I did not like it before, when he seemed to hold all the cards, but I like it even less now, him seeming a broken man, myself with the weight of knowledge.

"What about Littlejohn?"

"I'll look into it."

12.

The toilets come back to life with the sound of a million bullfrogs. This is how spring announces itself. Bubbles rise through the pipes causing water to slosh over the side. It happens throughout the facility at different moments as various lines free up. I am lucky. My bowl only belches. Other inmates experience violent eruptions, geysers of half-thawed feces spattering walls and floors. Yes, everything is once again "normal," but that is not the word I would use to describe the atmosphere either within the prison or my own self. I have not yet recovered from my sojourn in the Rubber Room. My brain operates more slowly. It lumbers. I forget, then forget what it is I am forgetting. Physically, too, I seem to have descended a step. I miss a certain liveliness to my movements. I keep expecting to find it is temporary, just a slow recuperation after being dosed by such powerful soporifics. So far, though, in the battered steel where we search out our likeness, I find a man who has summited a ridge and is now stumbling down into an unknown valley.

"Harms, 620003."

Lanza has resumed his normal duties.

I take my cup, prepared for the show, silently rehearsing how to best send the pills up into one of my head's several hidden crevices.

"What the—?"

It is empty. My name and number are on the side but there are no colored bullets of sanity-threatening chemicals.

"Guess he forgot."

"But I need my medication," I argue, somewhat paradoxically, figuring this must be a trap or test.

"One day without won't hurt."

"Wait! What about my orange juice?"

"What do you need it for, if you don't have any pills to take?"

"Son of a bitch," I mutter, left with nothing but the wax cup and Mbaéré's all-too-neatly-printed lettering. I crush it in my hand.

Nevertheless I sense that along with the physical and mental decline there is a gain, a compensatory wisdom. I am seeing the world as I have not. Actions, events, thoughts, resonate differently, set off strange harmonies. I understand now how we are all steeped in time. Simply by moving my arm I am taking part in a lifelong ritual, causing events to happen in the past and in the future, both here and a thousand miles away. It is some solace for the creakiness I feel when moving from a position held too long, or the strange resistance objects have when I try to comprehend them. I stare and stare but my attention beads on their surface. I cannot gain access. Put more simply: I have trouble understanding what "things" are.

This is particularly true in the yard, where I regard a plastic box as I would a geological formation.

It's for taking a dump.

Right, I confirm. Of course. Porta Potty.

That is the one positive change that has taken place in my absence. The yard is open for business. But I cannot see much evidence of remediation. There are blue plastic sheets on the walls and draped over the rooftops as well, held in place by a network of elastic cords. The poisons are still here, accumulating now behind makeshift barriers, grain by grain, preparing to overwhelm us. Wind has ripped a hole in one section. It flaps, emitting clouds of airborne toxins. The general effect is of an uglier, more hopeless world, but one we are again allowed to wander about in.

They rest over the graves of my ancestors.

I frown. It is still cold. We are inadequately protected against the wind, which only bears a hint of growing less severe in the slightly softened sunshine of . . . March? The dirt bordering the blacktop does not ring when your shoe hits it. Each snow-covered chalet drips.

Your ancestors?

This was once a burial ground.

I realize, in a slow, overcoming-rational-thought way, that Crow, after all these years, has answered on the same psychic wavelength. We are having a conversation.

His eyes, piercing the here-and-now, create for me a long-gone plot of land with tilting decaying wooden frameworks from which feathers and weapons hang. Birds perch on the makeshift shrines, black and heavy.

And now you got a bunch of temporary toilets there, I sympathize.

It's a desecration.

But what are the odds? I squint at how the two realities overlay and fuse. I mean of you being sent here, to the exact same spot?

It is no coincidence. I was sent here to cleanse it. To avenge the warriors lying underneath. To punish those who spit on their memory. That's what Carr did. He made fun of our traditions. He did the War Cry.

War Cry?

The sound we make when we ride into battle. As a joke. He put his hand over his mouth and went, "Woo! Woo! Woo!" Like in a movie. He did not know he was summoning up the spirits. They gave me strength. They told me what to do. And the other man, he tried to change me.

What other man?

The brown one.

Mitra? You killed Mitra?

He told me I would be damned for worshipping false idols. He tried to give me a bible.

You couldn't have killed Mitra. I was with you. We were sitting in the assembly hall, remember?

While you lay on the floor, afraid of the bullets and gas, I slipped away. Your eyes were closed. While you were trembling like a rabbit, I went hunting.

But how did you cut his head so clean?

A warrior is always armed, he answers enigmatically.

I look around and—it is only natural—edge farther away. Outwardly he is the same. He has not moved a muscle. I am making this up. But if that is so, then why not assume I am making the rest up as well? The walls, my awful deeds, the company I find myself in? Has my head gone as rogue as my hands? Am I just a collection of conflicting chemical reactions smelting away in the crucible of my skull?

You killed Mitra because he took an interest in your soul? I risk.

He turns to me. He has never done this before. He physically turns and pours his gaze directly into mine. Still his lips do not move.

The spirits told me to do it. You saw. You know the truth. You found the heart of the burial ground, where a warrior's soul rises. Remember? This world is just a passageway. The shadows are all in our eyes. Our true state of being is light.

You cut off Mitra's head because a dead Native American in a crapper told you to, I confirm.

I sent him back to his fellow devils, all of you who came here with your disease and filth.

Oh, like your people weren't just as big jerks when they had the upper hand on another tribe, I scoff, thinking, at the same time, my god, you are about to have your neck snapped.

Robidoux comes over. He shatters the sheath of silence that protects us. Ironically what he says is less easy to decipher than the hallucinatory offerings of my neighbor.

"What?" I frown, dragged unwillingly back to the primitive world of oral communication.

"—said he wants to see you."

"Who?"

He nods over his shoulder.

I turn to Crow, hoping to resume and build upon what we have just established. But he has gone back into himself so completely that it makes me doubt what I just experienced, that we actually took part in that most rare and fleeting of events, a moment of true connection.

Sacred? A burial ground? Out there? I ask silently, surveying the thirty or so snowbound toilets.

He shows no sign of hearing on any level, psychic or otherwise.

"C'mon," Robidoux grunts.

"Who wants to see me?" I repeat distractedly.

Despite that fear, I do not want to leave. I sense once I go I will not be invited to sit down again. Like most friendships, ours seems to have reached an unantici-pated crescendo, after which there will only be mutual embarrassment and an inevitable petering out.

Robidoux grabs my shoulder, pulling me by the sleeve.

I shake myself free but go with him. I do not look back. With every step I am retreating farther from the mystery, one I came upon by accident. But really how else does one discover things? Chance rules. I feel Crow's eyes but get no sense of what the intelligence behind them makes of it all, what he thinks of me.

The girl Mother told me about did not exist. I searched for her, hair in braids, plaid tights, too much makeup and, most of all, how she walked, like the Earth was new, only recently cooled. I discovered much about myself by how I looked at women. This was when I first began to formulate my theory that the eyes are on a separate mission from the rest of our being, that our goals only occasionally coincide. Mine burrowed deep into shapes, into slouches of posture, into color and texture, not just of hair, the bright sheen versus the more in-drawing glow, but such utter irrel-evancies as clothing. How could the eyes invest such significance in what would so soon be discarded? Is it women in purple I like? I asked. Or purple on women? I was a man led by dogs, a pack of them, straining at the leash, pulling me a hundred different ways, my heart in the middle, confined and aching.

It was her, of course. I realized that. Herself of many years back before she became, in her words, a tart or slut or worse. But any clue is better than none. Otherwise the search would be random. I saw how other people paired off. Clearly it had nothing to do with love. Often it was the exact opposite. I was determined to find some loose end, any sincere urge, it didn't matter what, gather it up and trace it back to its source. It was the beginning I was interested in, to untangle the initial knot, right the first wrong, so the rest could flow unimpeded and usher in a golden age. I wanted what everyone wants, to be happy.

Father Bryan's attempts at closeness only convinced me that clumsy groping was nothing more than a way to tamp down more serious desires. It was an excuse, an evasion. What he was feeling had nothing to do with me, not in particular. I could see it in the way his eyes were elsewhere, dreaming of their former home, out in space, while his stubby fingers plowed ahead, blind. They were moles, the very creatures he was afraid of, going through the motions, tunneling in the dark. This isn't going to be me, I promised. I am going to be invested. My expressions of love will exist in the here-and-now.

My declarations will be *serious*, I repeatedly swore, as the sweat from his nose stained the purity of my virgin skin.

That was my pathology, doctors informed me later. I took things too seriously. I wanted my encounters to be meaningful, whereas what I saw around me were people wallowing in tawdry, mass-produced fantasies, barely acknowledging the unique precious soul they ostensibly embraced. I wanted *her*. Whoever she may be. "Paraphilia," one psychiatrist smugly summed up, as if a fancy word could neutralize the power behind that simple logical desire. "Intense sexual arousal to an atypical situation." "And what's the cure?" I was foolish enough to ask. "There is none."

. . . which means it is not a problem, I refrained from pointing out, you sad, sexually unfulfilled, already-dead man. You are merely envious that I am alive. That is why you want to lock me up. I am a standing reproach.

The girl was her, and so, in searching, I went back in time. I became my father, the invisibility at the core of things, for who else had sought this girl out but him? And since I had him in me did it not make sense I was uniquely qualified to find her? It was that rare moment I spoke of before when the interests of the eye and mind intersect. I gathered up the past, wrapping it into a neat ball like string, not caring where it led, undoing history.

ROBIDOUX TAKES me to a corner of the yard far from the guards. It is directly under the tower so the marksman up high cannot see us either. The blue wrapping softens the edges of the place. I feel strangely calm.

"Why aren't you on your bench?"

"Privacy," Stanley whispers.

He has several followers with him, notably Shelburne, who has avoided me ever since my return. It is an awkward situation. Technically, Shel has the right to reshape my face since I "assaulted" him in public with no apparent provocation. But he also knows different, knows I was saving, not harming, him. Ironically this has elevated my status, such is the inverted ethos of the place. If the truth were known, that in a moment of weakness I risked my safety in order to protect someone who had been told to beat me, I would be reduced to a laughingstock.

"Let's make this quick."

I square up, offering him a free shot to even the score. It shouldn't, since we are not in full view of the others, but I am hoping the special circumstances only he and I know about will allow him to cut me a break. Otherwise he is more than capable of squashing me like a bug.

". . . not about that," Stanley answers.

Shel himself looks . . . I would say racked by indecision but that implies he is capable of entertaining opposing thoughts. Rather, he is *confused*, standing ramrod straight, arms at his sides, making fists more in response to the cold than as a show of anger. Robidoux, by contrast, lives up to his Gator nickname. He maintains a wide, toothy grin, waiting to scuttle forward and chomp whoever hits the ground first.

"You got something of mine," Stanley explains.

I inventory what I have, which is nothing more than a basic understanding of human nature.

"I thought the last place anyone would look was under that stinking Indian's ass."

"Don't know what you're talking about."

"Put it back."

"Can't put back what I don't have."

"It's just a piece of scrap."

"Then how come you want it so bad?"

"I hear the dryers in the laundry room still work. Maybe they'll find you in there."

"Won't get you any closer to what you're looking for."

Stanley stares. He may be crazy but like most crazy people he is not dumb. He has a goal and focuses on that, to the exclusion of all else. He nods. Shel takes a step forward.

"You OK?" I ask.

It is the same question I posed in the cafeteria. He pauses, fists half-raised, like a statue in a wax museum.

"He's going to take you out," Stanley warns.

"You do that, I might crawl into your head and inhabit your dreams," I speculate mildly. "Like that woman. The last one. What was her name?"

"Whore," he breathes unwillingly.

"Not enough of one apparently. She didn't do what you said. She didn't die."

"All right." Stanley prevents Robidoux, not Shel, from taking some kind of action.

"Even after you paid her," I go on. "Or was that the problem? Did you not settle up with her before? Is that why she would not go quietly?"

"Fucking bitch!" he screams.

There is an amplified squawk from the tower directly overhead. Stanley glances up. Shelburne is trembling, liable to cause a scene. One of the guards across the way is looking over. He is in danger of losing control of the situation.

"All I want is my property."

"What makes it so special?"

"Because I made it, that's why."

"Made it where? You got yourself a workbench?"

"Yeah. You, me, and a rack of power tools," he says dreamily.

His tongue makes a strange, medicated gesture, as if slurping some syrup.

I leave before they change their minds, pushing past shoulders, making for more public space. It is all about how you hold yourself. You got to keep your head on a swivel but at the same time stare straight ahead, act like you don't care. Never let them see what you're feeling.

Robidoux lobs something after me. It lands wetly, just off to the side. I try not to react in any way, all the time wondering what it can be. Mud? Spit? Or more of those deformed words his addled brain and squishy jaw can no longer fashion into sense?

It is still Cooney's cell. Like a dropped stitch in the fabric of things, it refuses to be filled. The resulting vacuum draws me in. I spend hours contemplating our relationship, a word I hate, though the others that present themselves, "friendship," "love," fare no better. If I betrayed him, did he not see it coming? Did he not provide me with means and opportunity? Did he not, on some level, want to be confronted with his crime? And whatever punishment he ultimately faced as a consequence, is not mine greater? To have ceased feeling, however briefly, alone, and then have that comfort taken away with no one to blame but myself?

But if Stanley thinks he is getting his tool back he is sadly mistaken. My fingers tighten around the slat's smooth length. I love how it responds to the minutest pressure. It is night. There are still sounds, yes, but not the rumbling matrix of rumors, lies, and threats. It is late. The air is thick with dreams. Guards on the night shift drowse in dimly lit Plexiglas booths sipping coffee

laced with alcohol. I get up off the bed. I do not bother
to open my eyes wide. I could just as easily leave them
closed. To say I am familiar with my surroundings
would be an understatement. I know the exact latitude
and longitude of every steel bar, each stumble-causing
rise of the cement floor, the placement of every grate,
the force lines of every crack. I slide the feathery blade
behind the bolt. Crisply the mechanism responds. The
door rolls back.

I take one, two steps. I fight the urge to retreat. A
sea creature without its shell, I feel a strange expan-
sion. I am physically assimilating my surroundings,
every pore taking in new space. I cross the row, an
unthinkable direction, neither left nor right, touch the
front of Cooney's cell as I would his shoulders, a frank,
sincere, manly greeting. We never touched in real life,
nor did I want to, but with this surrogate, my fellow
crustacean's former home, I have no trouble expressing
emotion.

Then I get to work. I kneel, feeling the lock from
the outside. It is different, of course. I do not know
if this will work. I can break out, but can I break in?
I must take what I have learned and reverse it, with
my mind's eye turn everything around. Minutes pass.
I keep trying, but find no way in. I scrape along, looking for where the crack should be, but find only confusing asymmetry. Unknowns keep getting in the way,
rivets and plates I cannot identify. I begin to sweat,
see myself as perpetually trapped, not free but not safe
either. Then I realize what an idiot I am. I simply reach
through the slot, where meals and mail are passed, and
manipulate the blade from the other side, forcing the
lock open as I would my own. It yields with the same

obliging click. I withdraw my hand, pull the door, and slip in.

Someone coughs, rolls over in his sleep. Another mumbles in semi-submerged language, responding to dream query.

"Where are you?" I whisper, reaching out, not knowing what I might find, not even realizing until now this is what I came to do: search. Search for clues. I touch every surface, collect psychic residue through my fingertips, run them over surfaces, his file boxes, his bed, no longer neatly made, the sheets and blankets carelessly replaced.

They took the nightie. Why would they do that? Does it mean he is still alive?

The space beneath the bed is empty. I wave my arm to confirm, but crawl under anyway. I need a quick sip of confinement, of walls pressing in on me, to quell the panic of being so far from home. It smells down here peculiarly of him, much more so than in the rest of the cell. I sniff, trying to sharpen a sense that, with all the noxious odors one must contend with, is more often stifled. Cooney, some pocket of him, like the air that lingers in an envelope, is still here. I feel all around. The frames are simple, with no springs that can be uncoiled and turned into weapons, just plain wooden planks. I am certain, with a crazy certainty, that I am close to something. I feel the mattress. My fingers slow down, encountering an unexpected anomaly. A section is impacted, has a density greater than that of its surroundings. Something is stuffed behind the cheap filler. I scrabble along the edge, far from the area in question, find a slit, barely there. I reach and after much coaxing extract a plastic box. If it is black in the cell, it is darker still under the bed. I turn the rectangular object all around, feel parts that go down and a hinged section that comes up. I press, at random, and go rigid as Cooney's voice booms out of nowhere:

"TRUST YOUR INSTINCTS! TRUST THEM TO BE WRONG!"

It is his cassette recorder. Frantically, I feel around, trying to find the volume.

"ADMIT DEFEAT; THEN BEGIN GUERRILLA ACTION!"

In any other place, the sheer loudness, not to mention the nonsensicality, would wake everyone within fifty yards, but here it just sounds like someone's dream made manifest, a comatose soul being forced to shout his demon's commands.

"IF YOU CAN'T BEAT 'EM . . . *BEAT* THEM!"

I finally find the Off switch, kill him in midsentence.

Absence makes the brain go softer, I ruefully admit, having forgotten what a jerk Cooney could be when he played the role of bad-boy guru. Finally acquainting myself with the controls, I reduce his proclamations to a whisper and play the rest of the tape up against my ear. It goes on for fifteen minutes or so, a rambling bunch of musings, seemingly unconnected. Apparently he was working on another book, not a sequel but philosophy, or what passes for such these days, mostly aphorisms, if you can call them that.

"IF ALL YOU THINK ABOUT IS SEX THEN YOU ARE NOT THINKING!"

The worst part, I frown, is knowing that it would have been a bestseller.

I try reinserting the machine and its precious contents back into their hiding place. Why did he bother to conceal them? The tape recorder is not illicit. He must have known he was being taken, known he would not be allowed to bring it along. But taken where? For what reason? I fit it snugly into position and work my way out from under the bed. Should I have rescued the cassette? What if they throw his mattress away one day? It will be lost forever, *The Revelations of Raymond Cooney*.

I let myself out, cross the row, and clang the bars to my own cell shut. Once the tool is stowed, I lie back, too amped to sleep. I stare, try to collect in my wide-open pupils a few crumbs of light. Yes, I know what is here, or thought I did, but now I would like to *see* it, see if anything has changed, take it in fresh.

What if he is right?

The question glows in the dark. Finding no response, it poses itself again.

What if he is right? What if he is a prophet? A genuinely wise man? What if that cassette is a sacred text?

I am cursed with just enough memory to reproduce Cooney's voice, its varying inflections from the different times and moods in which it was recorded.

"YOU SAY YOU'RE A FLY ON THE WALL? THAT MEANS THERE IS SHIT ON THE FLOOR!"

"OUR STORY TAKES PLACE IN A DYSTOPIAN PRESENT!"

"Shut up!" I scream.

Someone laughs. Is it him? Someone is awake, listening to my distress. I glare across to where his cell smugly exudes a continuing mystery, a mocking emptiness, and worry that I forgot to press Stop. What if the spools of that obsolete machine are still toiling away, if his muffled bits of fortune cookie poison are seeping into the atmosphere like the gas in old-fashioned exe-cutions? What if everything he says is God's honest truth?

"NOBODY LOVES YOU WHEN YOU'RE DOWN AND OUT IS JUST ANOTHER WAY OF SAYING NOBODY LOVES YOU!"

He laughs.

13.

It is odd, Stanley mentioning the laundry room, because that is where I next meet Mbaéré. He has been evicted from his Sick Unit, which is undergoing the same kind of ineffectual cleaning as the rest of the place. In the hallways this consists of nailing sections of plywood over the previously exposed networks of pipe and wire that compose our ceiling. Like the blue plastic sheets of the yard they are laughably stop-gap, not addressing the source of whatever is poisoning us, merely erecting a temporary barrier to delay for a few months or years the final reckoning.

"And then what?" I go on, not that he shows signs of paying the slightest attention. "They going to rip everything out of here and start over? What about us? How do they decontaminate us?"

There is a table set up, over which he has spread his papers and equipment. Several filing cabinets, locked cases, plus the ever-present gurneys are ranged against the round windows of washers and dryers.

"Of course it doesn't really matter to them. We're here for life anyway so what do they care if we die sooner rather than later?"

"There is the staff to consider," he contributes. "The health of the guards and administrators."

"I doubt the powers that be make that distinction, no offense intended."

"None taken."

He is staring at the contents of a folder.

I am loose, after a mild disagreement he had with the guard who brought me. Rather than sit on a gurney, I stand. This is not an examination. I have been summoned.

"We're just these pesky people who are still alive when it would make more sense to them, economically and conscience-wise, if we ceased to be. Think of it. They wouldn't have to pay you, wouldn't have to pay for our upkeep, wouldn't have to acknowledge why we're here to begin with, all of us, what our existence implies."

"Sit, Harms."

"I'd rather not, if it's the same to you."

I am speaking out of nervousness. One does not usually get called to see the doctor unless it is bad news.

"I have been examining the results of your tests, the blood I drew as well as the bone marrow sample I took."

"Bone marrow? When did you do that?"

"You would not remember. You were very heavily sedated at the time."

"You mean you did something to me while I wasn't even aware?"

"I had to rule out certain possibilities. It was during the aftermath of your most recent seizure."

"I didn't have a seizure. I saved a man from choking."

"You're sure you won't sit down?"

"Don't you need my permission to poke something into my spine?"

"Of course not."

He continues to stare at the folder, even though there are not that many pages to it.

"How come you stopped giving me pills?"

"I beg your pardon?"

"My medication. The trays. The last few days my cup has been empty."

"Yes." This seems to provide him with an unexpected way into whatever it is he means to say. "I did stop your medication. You have complained about it in the past."

"Since when does my complaining result in any action being taken?"

"You said it made you feel 'less yourself.' "

"Why am I here?"

Everything is wrong, the laundry room, stuffed with the apparatus of the Sick Unit; Mbaéré, instead of his usual cool, detached demeanor, acting human and hesitant; myself, trapped in a rising sense of dread, as if something life-changing is about to occur in a place where all change is for the worse.

"You do, in fact, have a condition," Mbaéré finally sighs, setting the folder aside, "which accounts for some of the abnormalities you have been experiencing."

Now I do want to sit, but not on one of the gurneys. I remember Stanley's threat and smile at how comforting it would, in fact, be to leave this world and curl up inside a still-functioning dryer, to bask in its warmth while going around and around.

"It's that nuclear power plant, isn't it? All those rays. And no one says a word. We just sit here getting mutated, act like it's in the natural course of things, like it's something we deserve."

"What power plant?" Mbaéré frowns.

"You're a foreigner. You're too naive. You can't imagine what people do to each other here. The lies they tell for money. They give us cancer just for the sake of a cheap electric bill."

"Cancer?"

"That's what you called me in for, right? I have a brain tumor."

"You don't have a brain tumor, Harms. Sit."

My knees, shaky enough already, submit to the gurney's padded surface. I half-expect the restraints to rise up of their own accord and bind me as in a horror film.

"Why did you think you have cancer?"

"You mean I don't? Are you sure?"

"You have epilepsy, Harms. That is what I've been trying to tell you. I've just had the results reviewed by a specialist."

"Epilepsy!"

"Surely you suspected something of this nature when you began to have seizures."

"I get the seizures from too much truth. It's not a disease."

"Epilepsy is a treatable, if not curable, condition," he lectures. "You will have to take anticonvulsive medication."

"For how long?"

"For the rest of your life. I am afraid that is no longer optional. Otherwise you would pose a risk to yourself and others. That is why I suspended your previous treatment. There are possible negative interactions to consider. However, with these new drugs, I think you will find your swings in mood much reduced."

"I don't have mood swings. I react to events."

"Once the chemicals from your previous course of treatment are cleared from your system, we can commence the new therapy."

"Dilantin."

"There are a range of options we can try. Depakote. Keppra. Trileptel. Some of these drugs are very promising in their—"

"—trying to turn me into a zombie."

"They are used by millions of ordinary people every day."

"I have no interest in being an ordinary person."

"They will stop you from swallowing your tongue."

". . . and seeing God."

"I thought you would be pleased."

"Epilepsy!" I still have trouble with the news. It is like a wave, crashing and then receding. "So it's got nothing to do with what I did? With my . . . missteps?"

"It is completely unrelated."

"What's the long-term prognosis?"

Mbaéré hesitates.

"It varies. If you respond to the initial treatment, you could lead a normal and . . ." He acknowledges the absurdity of the phrase. ". . . productive life. In a certain percentage of cases there is more extensive damage to the brain. An implant is used to correct electrical activity. For others, surgery is indicated. A cerebral lobe or damaged area is removed. It's a fairly straightforward procedure."

"What about my mother?"

He looks at me.

"Have you told her yet? She would come, if you told her."

"I believe your mother was contacted," he says carefully. "Or Warden attempted to contact her, rather, after your most recent episode. He was quite concerned. We never heard back."

"So that's when he dug up Father Bryan instead."

"Who?"

"The priest. The one who visited me."

From where I sit, I can see into one of the washing machines. It is luckier than I. Though useless, it still has properties, still merits consideration. Nobody condescends to it with pity.

"I am not aware that you had any visitors while in isolation."

"I didn't. Except for my old priest, Father Bryan."

This sparks Mbaéré's curiosity.

"You thought you saw someone?"

The rotting grapes. I briefly taste them again.

"Did you experience a hallucination? That would be interesting. Visions of that sort would be further evidence that you—"

"You really are a torturer." I understand, seeing the light in his eyes. "You're enjoying this, aren't you? Reducing me to symptoms."

"I am merely performing my duty as a physician, confirming my initial diagnosis."

"And maybe if I get worse they'll let you sharpen your instruments, open up my skull instead of my spine, carve out a piece of my brain. Perform a little elective surgery. Just like you did back home. Just like the good old days, huh?"

He smiles, revealing what I have never noticed before: a gold tooth.

I stare straight up. What is the ceiling but another wall? They call dinner. I do not go. Normally this would lead to cell extraction, a particularly brutal exercise of power. Guards forcibly remove you like a polyp that has rooted itself to some surface. They tear you "free," then beat you indiscriminately, kicks and sticks, as if it were a reasoned argument, trying to make you see the error of your ways. But that does not happen. Mbaéré must have spoken to them. The routine of prison life goes on all around me. The men leave. There is an interlude of peace, one I have never experienced before, the cells singing, each in a different pitch, their varying emptinesses. Then the trudge of return. Inmates ignore me, not knowing, but aware that a change has taken place. The way animals sense one of their own is sick. Yes. I am *sick*, I remember, once again trying to assimilate the news, trying to make it my own. Sick not crazy. I look over and see they have given me a boxed meal, just as they did with Cooney. Is this a sign? Did he know, the whole time, that a sentence had been pronounced on him as well? Is that why he would never tell me what was inside? I do not bother to eat. Gastric juices attack the lining of my stomach. I am dissolving from within.

After dark, after lights out, I listen to the voices. Their petty concerns. I can hear the guards too, their thoughts as they eat dinner with their families, watch TV, go to bed. I can hear Warden, his deep troubled "soul searching," a rather futile search, if you ask me. Mental blunting. Will I no longer be attuned to the universe? My respiration is reduced to quick, shallow breaths. I am the rabbit Crow saw, trembling on the floor.

I could write a letter, but to whom? Mother has taken herself away. She is deaf to my pleas. As for Dr. Bush, "Mrs. R. Lowenstein," the only topic she wants to discuss is one I have no interest in sharing, not out of shame or neurosis, as she would believe, but because it is a bore. It is all any outsider ever wants to talk about. You would think, from the barely repressed excitement with which they ask, they are envious of our crimes, the very horrors they censoriously agree we should be locked up for. Yet that is the sole event they are interested in. My sins are just excrescences, I try to tell them. Aberrations. There is more to me than bloodshed. But of course no one wants to hear how normal you are, how much you are like them. They get enough of that in their everyday lives. That is not why they go to the trouble of penetrating set after set of checkpoints, to sit across from "a fellow human being."

Epilepsy. A common condition shared with "millions of ordinary people." The death process has begun, the slow slide toward banality, toward a vacant acceptance. There is nothing I can say, no attitude I can assume, that will undo the damage or retard its progress. Nevertheless I yawn. Soon I will sleep, just like always. That is the worst part. I will go on as before. Outwardly there will be no change. Yet each act will be robbed of meaning. Instead of coming together to form a life they will be reduced to clutter. Everything will become artificial. Even dreams. How can a dream no longer have meaning? Yet that is exactly what the new reality brings. I have advanced as far as I can. The death process has begun.

"Who?"

"Dora Moody."

"I don't know a Dora Moody."

"She knows you."

Mail delivery is another of the coveted jobs that pays nothing but is still worth doing. It gets you out, provides social interaction, allows you to play Santa Claus, bestow gifts, even if most letters are from wives announcing unilateral divorce decrees or futile, aggressively worded bills from the very lawyer who failed to keep you out of here in the first place. I used to eagerly await mine. Then I was indifferent. Now I try to refuse, which is not as easy as you might think.

"I can't just take it back," Jabbar complains.

"Why not?"

"Wouldn't know where to put it. Nobody turns down mail. I might get in trouble."

"Open it yourself then."

"Not addressed to me."

"What are they going to do, arrest you?"

"Might lose my position."

He is very proud of it, straightening up to demonstrate, as if it is a real *position*, a picture that, along with the cart, will some day provide inspiration for a statue.

"Wait." The name does come back to me now. I regard with distaste the reawakening of my curiosity. "Dora Moody? Postmarked South Dakota?"

"That's right. You going to take it?"

He waggles the envelope through the slot. He does not let it fall. That would be a violation of etiquette. We are careful about such things. With so little under our control we pay extra respect to what remains. Dropping something into a fellow inmate's cell is a grave breach. I appreciate Jabbar's courteousness.

"You sure it's not for him?" I nod to the Raymond R. Cooney Memorial Vacancy across the way. "He's the one she used to write to."

"Mr. Ethan Harms. See? Don't get many 'Misters' around here."

Reluctantly I take it, along with a questionnaire some professor in Minnesota has obviously mailed to everyone in the penal system who committed two or more homicides. I resent being lumped with such amateurish riff-raff. It is not worth the energy it takes my molars to transform the paper back to wood pulp. Empty calories.

"Man, you really have an *oral fixation*."

"How's your cancer?"

He frowns, gives no indication of recalling our previous exchange.

"I don't believe you're sick at all. I believe you're all talk."

"Yeah? Well at least I don't eat paper."

"I'm just trying to get some intellectual nourishment. You talk a lot but you got nothing to back it up with. No experience. Hell, I believe you *are* wrongly convicted."

"Mail!" he scowls, understandably offended, and pushes his cart off.

Dora's letter is a wounded cry. She, I now remember, teaches kindergarten. It shows. A good teacher

is only a few steps in advance of her students, close
enough emotionally to still feel what they feel, while
offering a glimpse ahead, just slightly down life's
road, so both sides retain interest. I can see her with
Cooney, trusting, believing his protestations of innocence, the deeper, truer innocence of a man put on this
earth to suffer. The crude letters he wrote must have
affected her the same way a lopsided valentine from a
five-year-old with a precocious crush would. *My heart
went out to him*, she writes, and much more in that
vein. They even, apparently, spoke of marriage. I try
visualizing the ceremony taking place in an interrogation room despite the obvious evidence of the groom
already being pledged with steel bands on both wrists
and ankles to a far more demanding mistress. The only
detail that makes me certain she is not retailing some
perverted masturbatory daydream is his assuring her
she will accept his Oscar when the movie version of
Rocky Mountain Fever wins for Best Picture. That is
pure Cooney. *I have even been thinking about what dress
to wear.*

Thank god she didn't buy one yet, I think, trying to
guess a South Dakotan kindergarten teacher's salary.

*But my last three letters to Raymond have been returned
with no explanation. I called the penitentiary. When I told
them I was his fiancée, they said that did not give me standing to speak with anyone. Raymond told me something like
this might happen. He said if I ever stopped hearing from
him, I should write you, that you would know what to do.*

This is puzzling. I do not know what to do, not even
what he meant. Write and tell her that she will most
likely never see her betrothed again? Try and pick up
with her where he left off? She is not my type, nor I

hers. Teachers never interested me. I do not want to be taught. I want to learn. Or did he mean for her letter to provide me with a push, so I would not just lie here mourning in a vague way but oppose his disappearance and, in so doing, fight my own? He mocked me before for not seeing things, because if I did I would have to "act." Is that what he continues to do now? Is this his last message? Is he spurring me on to—as he did in our nighttime games—assert myself? Take matters into my own hands?

14.

Hygiene finally draws me out. Several days of immobility have neither made me more accepting of the news Mbaéré inflicted with such solicitous sadism nor presented me with an alternative course of action. I could lie here forever, suspended between hell and hell, or thought I could. But a week without showering is the most I can take. I strip away my soiled skin and line up with the others. They show no surprise at my reappearance; no welcome either. There is a deadness to the sleepwalker routine of the place that time away makes me more aware of, unless it is a pall I now cast being, in effect, a visitor from another land.

I am second-to-last in our row. I move into the spray and try experiencing each of the forty seconds as a distinct unit, a pearl on a string of pearls. I worship the lukewarm water, raising my arms, making ritualistic passes with the soap. The moment, within itself, lasts forever. I conclude, as one would a service, and move on toward the changing room, but hesitate, sensing someone's eyes boring into my back. I turn and find Littlejohn, his normally flat animal gaze alive with fury.

What? I mouth.

He has no response, just continues to try burning holes in me.

Remediation has made its way to the changing room. Previously bolted-down benches have been uprooted, lockers moved. An area beneath a particularly suspect patch of ceiling has been cordoned off. Seemingly no different from the rest, it invites speculation. Just what does the poison look like? There is no pollen-like dusting, no discoloration of tile floor. With the internal order of the place shifted, rows are interrupted, resuming at angles, so the guard assigned can no longer oversee everyone. He stands, as much a fixture as the pile of moisture-repellent towels, staring past the few bathers who do not bother to select a spot outside the range of his vision. The rest of us seek out our own little nooks and crannies. Asbestos can't be all bad, I muse, if it shakes up the place enough to allow for these unexpected enclosures of privacy.

"What the fuck are you trying to do?"

I jump. Littlejohn has come up behind and clapped his hand on my shoulder. He circles around, not letting go, his incongruously large penis brushing against my hip. He is dry, meaning he did not bother to take a shower but proceeded directly.

"I'm not trying to do anything."

"You're pissing me off, is what you're doing."

He positions himself front and center, blatantly confrontational. His manner is different from our previous encounters. Before, he only wanted to be rid of me. Now he blocks my vision, monopolizes it with startlingly alive blue eyes.

"You're not making any sense."

He grabs my chest hair and pulls.

"You talked to him. You told him you know."

"I didn't talk to nobody."

"You talked to *him*."

"The only person I talked to was—" It takes me a moment to understand. "I talked to Warden. About you. Yes."

He takes my hand. I am strangely limp, as if control of my limbs has been temporarily ceded. He plants it on his torso, where all the bruises bloom.

"You told him."

"I am trying to help you."

"He already knows, asshole. Stay out of my fucking business."

"What do you mean he knows?"

"You told him you know about us, about him and me."

"About him and you doing what?"

And then it becomes clear. So many things. Warden's martial arts training. Littlejohn's elevation to a prize job. How Warden's fingers have that way of worming their way into your flesh, and the violence behind his gaze, the lurking desire to do more than just touch. How he can break a board in two.

"Shit," I stammer. "You mean *he's* the one doing things to you? I didn't know. I wouldn't have told him if I thought— It was an accident."

"So's this," he nods, meaning what is happening right now.

We do not have pockets. We are not deemed worthy. But there are other ways to carry things. In your shorts, your shoes. Not to mention the irregularities of the body itself. There is no shortage of hiding places, in the mind as well, as his sudden take-charge attitude illustrates. I am not too surprised when he takes from his pile of clothes a half-used roll of duct tape. As I said, we are all magpies, hoarding abandoned objects.

"Where'd you get that? From one of the cleanup crews?"

His hand has somehow grafted itself to my nether-region. We are united. The strong response he coaxes from me is the result of loneliness, of deprivation rather than lust. It is just as paralyzing though. Root and branch, we are connected. Not just below, but in his eyes, and in the way my mouth, like the rest of me, has given over to a strange stillness.

"I don't have what I usually use," he apologizes. "So you're going to have to work with me."

It is not a person speaking. It is the alien. It is his eyes, the creature inhabiting them. They issue directly the sense they wish to convey. Words are poor approx-imations. I nod, to show I understand, but even that is an effort. I am awake, more so than ever in my life, but without authority. My only wish is—how did Mbaéré put it?—to comply.

He still has a firm grip on me underneath. It is not physical. It is deeper than that. What physical-ity refers to. He raises the role of tape to his mouth, snags the end with his teeth and unrolls a section. Its sound, the strong adhesive being activated, reverber-ates in my skull. For someone who claims never to have employed this method before he is remarkably sure-handed. Swiftly he loops the spool around the back of my head. Tape settles firmly across my mouth. The glue of it sinks down into me. A kiss. How long has it been since I was kissed? With those same sharp teeth he bites off the end.

"I can't believe you tried to take him away from me," he says, hurt.

I didn't, I answer.

It is a muffled cry, deep in a cave. Not a sound.

"What we have is special." His hand is still down below. Now the other reaches up to my nose. "He's mine. I'm his. He's going to have his fun first. That's part of the deal. Everyone gets to have his fun. And everyone gets what they deserve. That's how it works. He gets his, then I get mine. Understand?"

I nod. I do understand. It makes perfect sense.

"It's supposed to be slow." Again he apologizes. "Not like this."

I can feel his annoyance as he presses close and pinches my nostrils. It is the frustration of craftsman being rushed. All around there is sound, movement, but we are alone. I am in his gaze.

"I just have to shut you up. This isn't how I normally do it. But I'll make it worth your while. Besides it's what you want, right? It's what you've been asking for."

He begins to pleasure me. The strokes are in time with the amplified pounding of my trapped heart, in time with my attempts to draw breath where it is impossible, where, unbelievably, the everyday routes to life are closed off. Primal urges take over. My knees are shaking. Yet there is also in compensation the promise of relief, obscene relief. Perhaps I will finally be able to experience what others spend their lives in the pursuit and enjoyment of, what I have been denied. But is this the cost? I always suspected the two were one.

How long can you hold your breath? I ask. Three minutes? Four? Is that the length of a lifetime?

"You're going to have your fun," he promises.

It seems I will, if unwillingly. But before that happens, a hand takes his face and bashes it backward into the sheet metal locker. Something interposes, a wall of beef, not the veal calf of Littlejohn's pale body but red and thick and meaty. The grip on my penis is gone, as is the spell. He is giving the boy a quick, quiet beating, as one would a carpet hung over a porch rail, dense repeated blows. My nostrils are free, but I need more. My hands, alive again, claw at the lower half of my face and pull down the tape. I breathe in, the same raspy breath Shelburne took when I saved him. Now we are even.

"Boy," he says, delivering a compact swing to the gut.

Unlike Stanley, he does not confine himself to semilegal tactics. Using his bare foot, he kicks Littlejohn hard in the scrotum. I have never seen this otherwise familiar action performed naked-on-naked. It is transformed to something you might find on the side of a Greek vase.

"Boy," he says again, a strange insult or point to drive home.

"Fucking asshole," I manage to croak, more mundanely.

My voice is unrecognizable, a stranger's, with no personality or inflection.

Littlejohn lies still, either playing dead or dead for real. I could not care less. My interest in him has plummeted. This is what you get, or almost get, I chide, for trying to save others. So much for a ministry. Better to save yourself. I note with disgust how engorged my member remains. I would like to cut it off. It is the source of nothing but trouble.

"Thank you," I tell Shelburne.

His reaction is not what I expect. Not gracious at all. He gives a quick look in either direction and slams his forearm, like a bar, across my throat.

"Where is it?" he panics.

I try to indicate that I cannot very well answer if he too blocks off my windpipe. He lets me loose. My knees buckle. I begin sliding slowly to the floor.

"I *need* it." He hauls me up. "He says if you don't bring it to yard, *today*, he's going to gut me like a fucking fish."

"That's what I don't get. If it's so important to him how come he keeps sending you around instead?"

Shelburne pauses.

"Maybe because he doesn't want to get in trouble," I theorize. "Get himself locked away in isolation where he can't do whatever it is he's planning. And why *today*?"

He goes almost cross-eyed trying to follow my—or any—train of thought.

"What makes today different from any other?"

Shelburne smiles, unable to withhold secret knowledge.

"Because they're moving them tomorrow."

"Moving what?"

"I don't know." Nervous, he lapses into repeating what he was told. "Tomorrow. First thing. That's why he needs it *now*."

"I don't have it on me, for Christ's sake. Look!"
I spread my arms wide to emphasize my nakedness.
"What are they moving tomorrow, 'first thing?' "

"If I tell, will you give it back?"

This is his idea of bargaining.

"Sure."

"You promise?"

"At yard. I'll bring it with me. I promise."

"Swear!"

He is utterly sincere. It is almost touching, his child-
like faith in one's word, if you do not remember what
landed him here in the first place.

"I swear on my mother's grave."

"No more crappers," he reveals triumphantly

"You mean the Porta Potties? What does Stanley
care when they get rid of them?"

A guard appears. We have been making too much
noise, been out of sight too long.

"Fell," I say jerking my head down to Littlejohn.
"We were just helping him up."

He squints.

"What's that around your neck?

"Bandage." I plaster the loose tape back down.
"Doctor put it there. Didn't you hear? I'm sick."

We are both shooed out. On the way, Shelburne
confirms, with the first hint of misgiving:

"Cross your heart?"

". . . and hope to die."

OF COURSE I do nothing of the sort. I boycott yard as I
have done for the last week. Why should I go where I
am disrespected? I lie on my bed, much as Cooney did,

performing "mental calisthenics," exercising "within the limitless freedom of my mind." The guards no longer disturb me. They know, if not the particulars, that something is up with my health. I am allowed to go my own way. I am transcending this place, this prison of one's flesh and desires. I lie back and sift the pieces of knowledge I have collected. I do not have any specific goal in mind except understanding. The distractions—Warden's need to punish in a loving way, Littlejohn's craving for correction so he can lash out and feel justified in the gratification of his desires, my illness and the casual way Mbaéré promised to destroy my brain, Jabbar's empty boast that he is acquainted with death, Sweater Man and the money he represents, how it crushes the world, perverts nature far more gruesomely than the occasional acts of violence we inmates have performed, the invisible nuclear power plant and its cancerous radiation—all these gaudy bits and so many more fall away. What remains are the crappers, the Porta Potties, and Stanley's piece of metal, a tool he managed to find the right material for, then crafted, involving who knows how much trial and error, for a specific purpose. That is the truth fighting to shine through all this delusion. But why? A tool that can get you out of your cell but no farther. What was his motivation? There are gates, six of them, between the block where we spend our lives and outside. But between our cells and the yard there is nothing, just wide crash-bar doors passed through by hundreds of prisoners each day, for who would want to "break out" into there? It is a barren expanse, a killing zone, a walled-in square with guard towers and razor-tape-framed views.

And portable toilets. Just for now. For this unusually harsh winter. Which they will be removing, stack-
ing on the back of a flatbed truck driving through the
loading entrance, a high cut-out section of the far wall
I have never seen opened, tomorrow morning.

First thing.

Evening comes. I refuse dinner again. There is
activity all around me. I never thought of it as such,
the hustle-bustle of prison life. I thought of it as noise,
grating and debilitating. But now, generating my own
stillness, not relying on Crow's or Cooney's or anyone
else's connection to the deeper rhythms, I let it wash
over me. There is only one thing left to wait for and it
will not come until much later. Patience is something
I thought I had already acquired after so many years
here, but it turns out I have not truly learned that skill
until now. Night comes. I feel it, the rising tension of
the dream world. The buzz of pillow talk. Bait floats
past, topics to waste my mental energy on, but I take
none of it. I wait, so silent I am almost not here. And
then it happens, confirmation of what I have painstak-
ingly reasoned. Stanley's rule of the roost, his King of
the Jungle cry begins. But instead of the usual asser-
tion of supremacy, his call that swings from branch
to branch above the facility, it is a roar of rage. He
screams out at my not keeping my word to appear
in the yard, at my absenting myself from dinner, at
Shelburne's bumbling attempt to strong-arm me which
only resulted in unintended revelations. He knows I
know, that by lying here I am thwarting the plan he
has devoted his heart and soul to. He screams out inco-
herent threats. He feels his only chance slipping away.
I hear in the wordless snarls all sorts of heinous acts he

will perform on my person. I let him exhaust himself, and feel a corresponding rise in courage. The menacing yells die away. He whimpers, cries. People snore. Night takes hold. I get up off my bed.

It is not easy to leave.

I open the door. The tool is once more just a piece of metal. All its magic has been used up. I set it on the floor, take a few steps. Through the gloom, I look back. I have made a facsimile. Though I cannot see, I sense him lying there, a sausage-like lump of clothes, its "head" as empty as mine has been all these years, covered by a blanket, seemingly turned to the wall. I am not really leaving, I tell myself. I have left the part of me they care about behind. Resolving never again to look back I stride rapidly out, turning neither right nor left. I approach the doors to the yard. There is a guard station and a sleeping guard. I pay him no mind. I push one door open a crack and slip through. The cold night air, raw spring, hits me hard. I welcome it.

But I am not expecting the lights. I am a cave man scared by stars. Blinking. Irrationally afraid. They are bright, white-beyond-white, perched on top of a sniper tower at each of the yard's four corners. They do not imply a man, though, with a scoped rifle tracing my movements. They are in lieu of true attention. Tower duty at night is reserved for officers so traumatized by bad experiences they are relegated to a solitary existence with no interactions and so no potential conflicts. What they do up there is their own affair and most likely has little relation to vigilance. I walk out into the emptiness, determined not to run, which might attract attention; not to cower either.

Do not look up, I coach. Do not be dazzled.

My footsteps sound loud, echoing on the asphalt.
I cross the main area and exhale a huge sigh of relief
reaching the relative safety of the forest, which is how
the cluster of structures appears. Shadows welcome
me. I walk among them. There is so much fear. What
if Stanley is wrong? What if I am found here in the
morning, trembling, shameful?

I pull open a door. It does not matter which. All
of them, I now realize, contain the same secret passageway. Inside, I sniff appreciatively at the reek. My
hands reach around, familiarizing themselves. My feet
do the same. I take deep breaths. I have to know this
place. It will be my home for the next few hours. I must
make it truly mine. There is now a particularly gross
task facing me. They will check, not very thoroughly,
but they will look inside every Porta Potty before it is
loaded onto the truck. I know this for a fact because I
know their minds, how they operate. I have had nothing else to do all these years but study them. The door
will be opened and a head will poke inside. I must not
be here. I reach down into the hole below the seat. It
is hard plastic. I feel the rim underneath, entrance to
the chamber where the shit collects, and grip it with
all my strength. It does not yield. I readjust, to get a
better angle and put my will into it. There is a crack. It
sounds, in the silence, like an explosion. I freeze, waiting to hear a shout from a tower, the crackle of radios,
the thunder of hoofbeats. But there is nothing. Just a
unit, settling, I tell myself, and go on, pull loose the
fragment of plastic. It is the most liberating moment
I have ever experienced, to feel that first piece come
away from the whole.

The rest follow more easily. There is even a flimsy bar I never noticed before. To stop children from falling through, perhaps. I yank that free as well. I tear away at the narrow chute until it widens. As I do, the smell rises. It is not pleasant, regarded objectively, but what it represents is so exciting as to be almost sweet. When the opening is big enough I test it out, scraping my sides as I lower myself down. The area below is truly awful. I barely fit, have to squeeze myself in. But so be it. There is nothing that can deter me. I climb back out, hauling myself up through the ruined bowl of the crapper. With the lid down, it will look exactly the same. I sit hugging myself, truly hugging myself, out of the need for warmth, yes, but also with affection. It has been so long. I shiver and do not let go, the way you do when you meet up with an old friend.

Banging awakens me. Light streams through the cheap plastic. Walls glow. Dawn. There is a freshness to sounds. Voices are alive, not weary and worn as they will be later. I raise the lid and climb in. The banging moves away. False alarm. They are checking farther down the row. But I stay here, keeping the lid open just a crack to breathe, although truth be told the air is just as foul above as below. I hear footsteps all around, many men, not just guards. I can tell the difference. These workmen from the company have a robustness even to their sleepy shouts. My heart is beating madly, ready to break out of its chest.

One voice in particular makes itself known. Lanza's. Hardly a surprise. He is in charge, overseeing the removal. I duck down, writhe deeper, and try not to vomit. It is not just smell. It is touch and sight. Taste, too, and the amplified buzz of flies. Every sense is

offended. I do not go elsewhere in my mind. I concentrate, focus on where I am, on what is. This is the
best place on earth, I remind myself. It will carry me to
freedom.

The door opens for less than half a second. Direct
light penetrates even down here. Then it closes, sending a shiver through the frail plastic shell.

There is another interminable wait. I begin to panic.
What if they find me, the me of old clothes and balled-
up drawing paper? There will be a complete lockdown
and a thorough search. I am still below, painfully con-
torted, just my face positioned above the hole.

But they will not. I have not emerged for breakfast
in days. They will let me sleep. They no longer even
bother to look, passing my cell door. I have been preparing for this, though I had no conscious knowledge
it was going to happen. The universe coincided, the
way it does once or twice in your life. The key is to take
advantage.

There is a bump. Down, not up. That is the first
surprise. I am lowered, off what I cannot imagine. I
rock from side to side, trying to clutch something, to
find a stable outcropping to grab hold of but there is
only cold shit. With no warning we shoot skyward. It
is the feeling of a roller-coaster or elevator, how a child
reacts when he is still new to the lurches of the world.
I swoon. There is a collision. My face bangs forward
into the ring of the seat. My lip is bloodied. I want to
cry out and forcibly clamp shut my jaw.

Then nothing.

Another eternity of waiting! I almost weep. Finally
loaded on the bed of the truck, here I am, going
nowhere! Other units are placed in position. I hear the

groaning of the small forklift that handles each with the same rude incivility it treated mine. A chain is dragged around the outer edges. It saws against the sides of my cage. Is there really going to be any difference, I begin to wonder, from where I am going and what I am leaving behind? The sun grows stronger. I can see it trying to burn through the roof. And still I sit. The tension becomes intolerable. Once more I fall asleep.

Weary, my head down, I am jolted by a different kind of motion, the slosh of packed units realigning themselves as the truck's brakes disengage and we ease forward.

I did not hear the gate open. I missed it. The big moment! There must have been a shriek. It is not used often. The doors are massive, to accommodate large vehicles. I heard nothing. I was dead to the world. I hear now the engine working its gears. We are rocking on waves. It is the difference between dry land and the sea, which I have never seen but am now launched upon, that vast ocean that lies beyond our atoll of brick and wire. We pick up speed. The units travel within their confined space, slam into each other, giddy, hysterical with excitement. Even these inanimate objects sense the change. A brisk breeze infiltrates the cracks of the walls, wafts through the ventilator baffle up top. Morning does its best to chase away the stink.

I am terrified. I have no business being here. I am not part of the natural order. That is what I have been told my entire life. Plus, a more immediate concern: I cannot stay. I cannot luxuriate in my shit-smeared chrysalis. They will find me eventually, the fake me, see I am not one of them anymore. The truck will be stopped or its destination surrounded. I have to get out, which proves difficult. The door opens inward, but I am still wedged next to another unit. There is no space. You have to make it, I tell myself. You have to make space where there is none. I crawl into the seemingly nonexistent area where one wall meets another. Each side gives slightly. I push forward. I am forcing myself up, just a few feet, to where the sun shines. I can feel the warm. It inspires me. I push. All that my body has been through comes into play. I am lubricated with fear. I have been sweating. I have been soiled. And now I am made strong. My head emerges. I give a yell. It is not heard over the roar of the truck and, besides, who else is there in this world but myself? I work free, extract the last bit of reddened foot from the maw of two flush walls, and lie panting on top, too exhausted to even notice for a moment what is going on, where I am.

It is country. Miles and miles of deserted land. We are on a road but there are no buildings, no trees, just the occasional line of scrubby bush and then more stretches of unforgiving red stone. To be stranded in the middle of all this with no clue how to proceed would be pointless. I fight with every argument my brain can muster the animal urge to jump, to disassociate myself from the last remnants of the place I have left behind forever. Even the Porta Potty, my agent of delivery, I regard with the disgust only a former home can incite. All the awful memories lie festering there.

It is still early. There are few other cars on the road. I flatten myself when one goes by. A stranger, noticing, would probably take me for a worker delegated to ride on top of the flatbed's load. "So as not to stink up the cab," I rehearse explaining. I am mesmerized by the undulating nature of the roadside, how the rock and cliff faces rise and fall in no perceptibly repeated pattern. It is endlessly fascinating, but I do not have time to be fascinated. I force myself to think. Time! Time is happening and I must stay ahead of it. We come to a gas station, one of those convenience stores with pumps out front and a large sign, visible from miles away. The sign gives me enough advance warning to scramble as close to the edge as I can get, hanging lower and lower, until I let go. For one moment I believe I will land on my feet and somehow pick up the pace of the truck, just run alongside until my sprint slows to a casual, winded walk. Of course what happens is I land hard, seriously injuring my shoulder as I roll on the pavement. It takes several minutes for the velocity of the flatbed to wear off. I hit surface, first road then, managing to veer, gravelly margin. When I finally stop, I lie stunned. Can this be what it feels like to be alive? I get up and examine myself. I am in working order. Adrenaline is dealing with the pain. I acknowledge all my wounds. They are there. I postpone feeling them. The convenience store is still a good thirty yards off. I am more interested in the small parking lot adjacent. It extends to the edge of a drainage ditch though there is no moisture in it at the moment. Staying low, I make my way, crawling down the far side of the embankment so as to be invisible from the glassed-in front of the store. A man or perhaps a boy is working the register. My eyes are weak. They cannot deal with so much sun. I crouch, waiting for the exact right moment. I must will it into existence. Cars come, for example, but park too close to the store. Or they gas up but do not park at all. I resist the urge to go off half-cocked. I bide my time. I remember Eldridge's words and let the game come to me. My metabolic rate slows to that of its surroundings. Birds understand. They fly over and cheep out notes of encouragement. I let my mind go blank. Soon it will be filled.

The car is not a model I know. It is a new one, or new to me, rather. Even the color, soft green, as if milk has been poured into the paint, is unfamiliar. I watch her get out but there is really no need. It was meant to be. Her shoes, low sensible heels, a receptionist, perhaps, on her way to work, or some boss lady at a minor concern, tell me all. Their click-clack starts the machinery in my body moving again, as if they have entered a code. All my DNA begins to replicate. Billions and billions of new me's crowd my bloodstream. I climb halfway out. Her car provides a barrier behind which to hide. There is another aching wait. The last, I promise myself. The heels, returning, plot points on a graph, illustrating her progress. I take a deep breath— my first ever—and step out at just the right moment, as she has her keys ready, bag slung over her shoulder, other hand balancing a little cardboard tray with coffee. Three cups, I note. For the office.

"Morning," I say.

It is not her. It is not Dr. Roberta Bush. That would be too perfect. But I show her anyway. I show her what I did. She wanted me to tell her, that is why she gave me her address, but I haven't the time to visit and, besides, telling does nothing. Telling is instead of doing. I fear Dr. Bush will not become much of a scholar. Her investigations are not bold enough. Had she really been interested she would have come herself instead of sending this poor woman in her place, this substitute who, like all of us, pays for sins not her own. I make short work of her. The car, its milky green, provides cover. I look up at one point and see, yes, it is a boy, staring aimlessly, as I so often did. Dreaming. Blood courses down and away, rushes toward the drainage ditch, obeys the lay of the land. It is with a deep melancholy rightness I sink my teeth into her flesh, nimbly avoiding the mess below. All the years of making do with substitutes, institutional food, letters, "pumpkin pie," are forgotten. A great joy spreads through my limbs. I forgive my persecutors. I attain mindfulness.

Her bag, off to the side, has a fair amount of money. How far will it take me? I am unfamiliar with the price of things these days. No doubt I will be scandalized. I find her key, roll what is left of her into the ditch, and start the car. I have no definite goal in mind with the time left me. Maybe I will drive south, to Florida, get out and walk into that swampy preserve from which our ancestors crawled forth a million years ago on their doomed journey, stand there until a huge, gray, grotesquely misshapen monster—but beautiful and generous and *loving*—rises up out of the water, the prehistoric creature who knew me way back when, who has been here the whole time, waiting. My manatee.